I0553272

FINDING
BIG FLAT

SAM PEMBERTON

Copyright © 2023 Sam Pemberton
All cover art copyright © 2023 Sam Pemberton
All Rights Reserved

No part of this book may be reproduced or transmitted in any form or
by any means, electronic or mechanical, including photocopying,
recording, or by any information storage and retrieval system, without
permission in writing from the author.

Other Publications by Pemberton
The Moonshiner and the Preacher
Livin' Under Goldie's Rules

Editor – Nancy B. Dailey
Publishing Coordinator – Sharon Kizziah-Holmes
Cover Artist – Sandi Lemarr

Paperback-Press
an imprint of A & S Publishing
Paperback Press, LLC

ISBN -13: 978-1-960499-08-0

DEDICATION

Finding Big Flat is dedicated to the families, and their descendants, who made the trip from Tennessee to Arkansas. They are the people who made this story, and regardless of where they live today, Big Flat remains their home.

If one of your ancestors went to school in one of the little schools at Cozy Home, Cedar Creek, Round Mountain, Cedar Grove, and others in the area, your roots were eventually in Big Flat, Arkansas.

The renovated building, now called The Gathering Place, and the museum portion, in Big Flat are dedicated to the memories of these same people.

The senior class pictures from Big Flat High School and Tri-County represent the families and people we want to honor with this dedication.

The author, Sam Pemberton, and his wife, Pat Pemberton, are part of the Class of 1962.

ACKNOWLEDGMENTS

I'd like to give a big shout out to Sandi Lemarr. You did a heck of a job capturing my vision of the cover. Thank you for putting your time in on this project. I appreciate you.

To you, Nancy Dailey, what would I have done without you? Your typing and editing of this book made it come to life. Thank you for everything. I look forward to the next project. You're a pleasure to work with.

Sharon Kizziah-Holmes, what can I say? You are the one that pulls it all together. You are the best publishing coordinator any author could ask for. I'm glad I finally found you after years of looking for someone to help with my books. Thank you.

Last but not least, thanks to my wife Pat. Thanks for putting up with the hours I've spent working on this story. You not only put up with me, in doing the last minute proofing of the book, you find all the little things others don't. Thank you, honey.

CHAPTER 1

It was cold in the tent. Ethan Massey had been awakened by the wind blowing the flap of the tent. Noah Sitton, his partner for several years since they went to New Orleans with Col. Jackson was snoring loudly. Between the flapping of the tent and Noah's snoring Ethan was not able to go back to sleep.

Ethan lay in the tent thinking about the letters he had written back home. It had not been easy sending mail. It was an involved process since the mail traveled with the pack mules bringing supplies for the survey crew. The pack mules with supplies came from the North rather than across the swamp while the mail was supposed to be delivered every 30 days it was closer to two months. And then, since there were several crews, the mail was often delivered to the wrong crew. Mail sent out usually took close to three months before it was delivered to their families in Wayne County Tennessee.

Of the four young men who had left Wayne County Tennessee to join the survey only Ethan Massey and Noah Sitton were left.

Ethan thought about losing Andy Rhodes and Jim Campbell. He had written the letter describing how Andy fell to his death while trying to plumb bob the line of the survey.

Andy's death occurred two years after they started the survey. Ethan remembered when they traveled to Memphis to enlist in the project. They ranged in age from 16 years to 23. Jim Campbell was the oldest and Noah Sitton was the youngest.

They were excited about helping survey the Louisiana purchase. The adventure of exploring had drawn them in. That plus the promise of free homesteads for everyone who was a veteran of the war of 1812.

The survey officially began in 1815. It was delayed by the war between the British and the United States which ended in 1814. The Battle of New Orleans was fought two weeks after the peace treaty was signed. The communications were slow just like the mail service for the survey.

The earthquakes starting in 1811, devastated the area along the banks of the Mississippi River. The ground sank in places creating bluffs. There were severe landslides in other places. Everything about the Mississippi River in the Memphis area and north of there was changed by the earthquake. The river still had not established its new channel in 1816 when the Wayne County boys joined the survey.

Ethan continued to stay awake recounting the loss of Jim Campbell. Jim Campbell had not returned to camp one evening. He had been trimming the site line for the survey along with one of the slaves. Gossip among the camp was that Jim and Zeke, the slave contracted from a plantation, left with two young Indian maidens. Reporting Jim missing was not a problem because there was hope he was still alive living with an Indian wife.

Ethan left the tent and was walking around the area they had camped for over five months.

His thoughts returned to when the survey started at Memphis. It was no easy task to cross the Mississippi River. They had to transport all their equipment, tents food and other supplies across the river. They had loaded their gear and equipment before attempting to load the pack mules.

Ethan Massey became the leader by default after Jim Campbell didn't return. Ethan replaced him as the chief among the three Wayne County boys. Andy Rhodes fell off the bluff before Jim and Zeke left the survey.

Nothing went as planned from the time they loaded the gear onto a barge, then unloaded onto a spot of land due east of the starting point for the survey. They found themselves in a snake infested swamp covered by a thick brush with other vegetation growing underneath, making it almost impossible to start their work.

Ethan was trying to visualize where their camp was in relation to the starting point of the baseline survey. The baseline was an east-west line established in the center of Arkansas parallel to the Mason-Dixon line which was being completed between Missouri and Arkansas.

Ethan's mind drifted back to the difficulty of not only communicating through the mail but with keeping track of their location. He was trying to visualize where they were. The problem with remembering was because the terrain changed back and forth so much. They started in a snake infested swamp covered by thick brush with other vegetation growing underneath. This made it all most impossible to start the survey.

They established the starting point at the intersection of the fifth meridian, Ethan only remembered it as being somewhere west of Memphis after they crossed the

Mississippi River.

The boys from Wayne County were encouraged by their folks to join the survey crew to scout out the best possible land available for settlement in the new territory.

Their families were part of a group of immigrants who left Europe to come to the US with a dream of being able to own land. Since their arrival on the eastern shore close to Jamestown they had been in a continuous search for the perfect spot to settle. The promise of free homesteads in the land known as Arkansas to every veteran of the war of 1812 helped lure them in to the survey.

As Ethan continued his walk after leaving the tent, he observed the area around the camp. He had named the place Big Flat. The name was a natural. A good description of the area with fresh water flowing from a spring in the middle of a huge amount of flat land.

Ethan remembered how proud he was when they climbed out of the hills and hollows and came to a spot where he could see for some distance. He also remembered how good it was to get away from the mosquitoes. There also was no fear of being greeted by a vicious cottonmouth at every step. The rattlesnake and the copperhead around the camp were poisonous snakes but they left you alone if you left them alone. The cottonmouth was different. It is territorial and will attack when you come in to their territory. This area was much better than the swamps.

Ethan considered how he was going to describe the land they had surveyed. There was open land beneath huge oak trees in the area around their last camp site. They were finished with the survey. This location was filled with plenty of game for food along with clear streams filled with fish. The terrain in Ethan's eyes was beautiful with the bluff's surrounding the open valleys. Before you could enter a valley it was necessary to climb through rough mountains. He tried to visualize how they would manage to cross the Mississippi River into the broken mess of swamps and trees left from the earthquake and then find their way along the streams until they came to a place where they could climb the hill and settle at Big Flat.

Ethan went back to his tent he had made a decision when he got back to Wayne County he would present Arkansas to anyone who would listen as an opportunity for a new land. But, only if they came early, and chose wisely. It would be hard work.

CHAPTER 2

The cool night air of early September, the soft sounds of the night with most of the wild animals along with the mules settling down. It still was not quiet enough for Ethan to fall asleep.

"Are you asleep?" Ethan asked. The tent was filled with his partners' snoring.

Noah Sitton stirred from his sleep, and finally sat up looking at Ethan.

"What are you doin' awake? Noah asked with irritation in his voice. "We've got to get some sleep. Tomorrow will be a hard day."

Ethan paused and thought before he answered. Why was he awake? He was anxious to finish the survey and start the trip back home to Tennessee. But when he thought of the journey home he could not visualize the trip ahead of them.

During the survey Ethan had been on the end of the chain that marked the distance along the line the surveyor was shooting at the time. Noah had been responsible for holding the pole and placing it on the line as directed by the surveyor. Ethan's job was to advance to the point at the bottom of the survey pole and hold the chain hard against it marking the spot, while Andy Rhodes continued farther up the line.

Ethan thought back to the day when Andy Rhodes had fallen off the bluff. He had extended himself with the chain in his hand out over the edge of the bluff trying to stay online and drop a plumb bob down the bluff to mark the spot where the line would continue. Ethan had lain awake several nights asking himself if he had relaxed the pressure on the chain, enough that allowed Andy to fall to his death?

The answer would not come. He could not be sure. Some days he could soothe his conscience by believing Andy had just slipped and lost his footing. Other days he seemed to remember losing his concentration and jerking the chain.

Ethan had a lot of reasons for not being able to sleep this last night in the tent.

I don't feel any guilt about Jim Campbell. He left camp with enough ammo to kill a couple of deer or something else for camp meat. We never saw him again. We never saw the Indians, either. The Indian maidens could have come from a couple of tribes. The survey crew came in contact with several Indians since they began surveying the mountains south of the White River.

"Why did you wake me up?" Noah asked, still irritated.

Ethan was startled by the question. He had no idea how long he'd been lost in his thoughts. Ever since they finished the survey and it was time to go back to Tennessee, he had spent a lot of time trying to decide how they were going to tell the families about the last three years.

The survey had been difficult. If there was open ground, it was filled with water and a mixture of snakes, mosquitoes, and Lord knows what else. But the majority of the work was hacking a tunnel through the brush. A clear line of sight was necessary for the surveyor to get a shot of the pole establishing the survey line.

Along with the four boys from Wayne County Tennessee there had been a total of ten colored slaves hired by the engineer under a contract with a plantation. Ethan thought about how these men had been treated ever since the time they loaded the equipment and got ready to cross the Mississippi. Any undesirable chore was given to the colored people. Most of the slaves had cooked their own food and stayed in a lean-to next to the wagons from the beginning of the survey.

While they were in the swamp keel boats were used to transport the wagons. The wheels were taken off and the tongue of the wagon placed in the bed and then the wagons were loaded on the boats. When they reached land dry enough the wagons were re-assembled, the keel boats would be loaded onto the wagons, and when they reached the next swamp the process would be reversed and once again the boats would haul the wagons. It was very tiresome going back and forth from boats to wagons during the travel through the swamps.

Ethan thought back to Tennessee and how few slaves were owned by the families in Wayne County. The Stennet family had maybe four total.

In the last three years he had gained an appreciation for the slaves. They were the best workers and never voiced a complaint. Ethan had inquired about that, asking them why they never complained.

"Mister, if I complain I would've been sold!" the colored man told him with wide eyes and an expression that told Ethan all he needed to know.

Noah had gotten up and began packing the stuff in the tent. Once again he interrupted Ethan's thoughts.

"If I'm awake I'm going to stay awake and get things ready to go in the morning," Noah stated.

Ethan began helping pick up stuff and packing. But his

thoughts continued. He remembered the day Andy had fallen off the cliff, and how the colored guys worked their way through a gap in the bluff back to the area where Andy was laying. They had found an area where it would be possible to get all their equipment down to the point where they could come back and pick up the line. It was almost half a mile to the east before they had been able to cut a trail off the bluff when they heard Andy had fallen.

"Why did you let Andy try that?" They were very upset.

Ethan remembered the question as he continued to pack. He had never been able to answer it.

They made a lot of progress with getting their packing done. Ethan didn't intend to unpack anything until he got home. He would sleep in a sleeping bag and roll it up and tie it behind the pack on the mule.

CHAPTER 3

The trail was easy to follow. It was an expansion of a game trail they followed when they first came upon the area Ethan had named Big Flat. As they began the trek home over the sandy trail, it had grown larger with each trip they made to start the next day's survey. Starting home was not nearly as exciting as Ethan imagined when he realized they were finished and ready to go home.

During the survey they had lived well with plenty of meat and other fruits of the land. They had traveled with another crew until they reached a point somewhere north of the White River. They had started working in two crews to finish the survey on time. There were times Ethan and Noah's survey crew reached the Mason-Dixon line before returning to the camp.

Ethan continually looked at mountains and different landmarks as they prepared to leave and during the first couple of miles along the trail. He turned and stared at the mountain that rose above the flat land a few miles west from where they were. It occurred to him that it was a pretty little round mountain. In 1819 little did he know his thought would one day become the name for that mountain. Round Mountain, as it became to be known, was the marker Ethan chose for his return visit.

The boys who left Wayne County to join the survey crew became friends with all the other people working with them. The strength of the party depended on the crew getting along and understanding their chore.

Ethan remembered the calmness of the engineer and the two colored men who were responsible for carrying his equipment. Ethan had looked through the transit several times just to observe the surroundings around them. He never touched any of the adjustments, nor did he ever help with the leveling and positioning.

"The best crew I've ever had," was always the engineer's comment after the two slaves would finish setting the transit over the exact spot the engineer had chosen.

Ethan questioned how the engineer planned to reward the colored men. Their freedom? They were a group of ten when they left Memphis, and about the same time Jim Campbell disappeared, one of the slaves had come up missing also. While the boys from Wayne County were experienced ex-soldiers who had made the trek with Jackson to New Orleans, the survey was not on a military mission. The engineer never discussed dropping the survey to try to find either Jim Campbell or the slave who left about the same time.

Breaking camp and starting home was easy. It was like the mules and the men realized the job was over. While the feed supply had been a problem with the delivery of grain, and other supplies being sporadic, the mules had learned to forage on the native vegetation and were in very good physical condition.

They had two wagons left, salvaged from parts of the

other wagons during the course of the three years they had been there. The wheels were a hodgepodge of emergency repairs, but they still turned as they rumbled down the steep hills. The flat was left behind them with the little round mountain disappearing over the horizon.

Noah Sitton hurried to catch up with Ethan. "Are you anxious to get home?" he asked.

Ethan stopped. "It's too early to even think about home." He stared toward the East. The sun was almost directly overhead. It had taken much longer to load up and start their journey than anyone planned.

"We've not come three miles yet," Ethan added.

"How long do you think it will take for us to get there?" Noah asked.

"How in the world would I know?" Ethan sounded irritated.

Ethan thought about the times he had watched the engineer post in the field manual from the notes made during the day. He also observed the notations and markings that were made on the map being used to plot the survey. He remembered the engineer's disgust when they had surveyed for two days and did not come to a stream noted on the map. "Somebody will have to reconcile these maps with the survey," had been the comment of the engineer each time he had placed the manual back in the case for safekeeping.

They had walked far enough that it was time to let the mules rest and drink from a small stream crossing the trail.

Ethan watched as the bubbles formed from the little stream falling over the rocks, and tried to visualize the directions the streams had run during their survey.

There was a creek not far from where the mules stopped that Ethan had nicknamed the Big Creek. He had no idea how many little streams culminated their journey into that creek. Then the creek wound its way down to join a river whose Indian name, he had been told, meant Buffalo.

"Noah, do you think this water is headed to the swamp we crossed below Memphis?"

"Ethan, I was lost when we got to the banks of the Mississippi, and I've been lost ever since," Noah answered.

Three years of continuous camps being moved, and then trying to stay on a straight line through a swamp, saw briars, trees hanging low enough that all the limbs had to be trimmed back in order to see through the transit.

"I don't know if lost is the right word," Ethan said. "What's bothering me is when I get back to Wayne County, our folks are going to expect us to know more than we do." His comment expressed his frustration with trying to get a clear picture of where they had been.

He remembered back in history class when their teacher had made the comment about Cristopher Columbus who started out not knowing where he was going, got there and had no idea where he was. He returned not knowing where he had been. And he had done it on borrowed money from the Queen of Spain.

Ethan laughed. It was the first time he'd seen any humor in their situation.

Noah laughed with him. "I'm so glad to hear you say that, because I am worried about the questions we're going to be asked.

"How are you going to describe it?" Noah asked.

"If we ignore all the bad things, they'll turn back if they decided to come." Ethan paused. "If we just talk about all the good water in the streams, the fertile little patches of land, and all he good timber with lots of game...." He paused again. "I don't know how to describe Arkansas."

A mix of good and bad he thought. The piles of rock along the streams that fallen out of the bluffs over the years as the streams had cut their way through the hills after leaving the mountains of north Arkansas. These large boulders had diverted the water back and forth between the bluffs, leaving bottomland opposite the bluffs.

It was different from the hills of Tennessee, but it was still similar.

How would he explain to his family that there would be a farm south of a stream, but you would have to cross it to visit your neighbor because their land would be on the north side?

"I believe we tell them it's a snake infested swamp until you get to the hills, and then it's a rock pile with briars," said Noah, "but if you can climb through the rocks after making it through the swamp, it's a wonderful place."

His comment brought a smile to their faces.

They crossed the creeks several times as they made their way to the banks of the Buffalo River for their first camp on their way home.

CHAPTER 4

Breaking camp was easier this morning than the days they had spent surveying. The mules' packs had been removed for the night while the mules were tethered to the rope line. It was simply a matter of strapping the packs on their backs and they were ready to go. Fresh meat was part of the cargo and would be a delicious meal later in the day.

It was September 1819, the year Arkansas became a territory of the United States. The Buffalo River and the mouth of Big Creek had not yet been named. Nor had the counties of Marion, Searcy, and Baxter been created out of the Arkansas territory.

Ethan woke up with a bit of anxiety, trying to mark places in his mind along the trail for the return trip.

"Noah, you see anything that would remind us to turn up this creek when we return?"

Noah looked back the way they had come, then turned to the north, observing the flow of the larger stream as it came out of a deep pool and rushed by for the smaller creek to join its waters.

"I think I can remember the tall bluff," he said as he

turned toward the east. "And I think I can remember the way the stream looks." He pointed at the water rushing out of the deep pool and flowing toward where they stood.

Ethan slowly turned, making the same observation as Noah. "I believe I can, too."

They joined the rest of the crew to finish loading for the day's trip.

As they began their trek along the south bank of the larger stream, the Buffalo River, they immediately saw a problem. The water rushed into a large pool beneath the overhanging bluff and came out in a circle tightening into a spiral at its center. The water built up in a crescent around the spiral and then rushed off the edge, dropping down in a rapid flow disappearing out of sight among the willow trees.

The engineer leading the group turned back and said, "Fellows, we have to cross somewhere else."

He walked slowly back up stream looking at the water, observing what kind of bottom there was in the river.

"We can't cross on that slick rock bottom." He continued walking upstream until they were immediately below the large pool.

"We just as well backtrack and find a crevice where we can climb out of this hollow and get on one of the ridges that I remember when we were surveying."

Ethan felt his spirit drop. It was disgusting to start the trip home and immediately find themselves having to reverse course for a better path. There had been so many times during the last three years when they'd come to a swamp that they couldn't get across because of the bog and the quicksand. Other times while they were surveying it had been almost impossible to keep the equipment with them along the line of the survey. Ethan shuddered when he remembered Andy falling over the cliff somewhere to the west of where they were now.

The sun was beginning to set. A fire had been built and

the meat harvested earlier was roasting. Almost ready to eat. The excitement of going home was now tampered by the problems trying to cross a stream which wandered wherever it chose.

They broke camp the next morning at a point where a stream almost as large as Big Creek joined the Buffalo River. It was déjà vu. Same as yesterday. They loaded the mules and discussed a plan. The engineer pulled out the maps and his survey notes, trying to determine where they were and what the best route would be.

"We should've paid attention when the supplies were delivered," said Ethan becoming more frustrated. "We may never make it out of Arkansas."

Ethan looked at Noah and realized his partner of over three years was almost at the point of tears.

"We will make it," Noah interjected. "We can always do like the fur traders." He paused. "We can build a raft, load what we want on it, and go down river." He pointed south. "We know what's down river, we went with Colonel Jackson all the way to New Orleans."

Everybody laughed. But they knew they had to make it home with the mules, the equipment, and everything that had been recorded about the survey.

The ten slaves that had started the trip were now nine hard-working men, considered comrades. They had huddled together during this morning's discussion. Their leader approached the engineer and talked as he pointed at the river.

Ethan got close enough to hear the conversation and listened intently as the colored man described how they could cross the river by stretching a rope or using the survey chains to create a line to hold everything in place, including the mules, while they crossed the strong current.

Ethan went back to Noah and said, "He has a real good idea," pointing to the colored man.

"He's the smartest guy on the trip," Noah said very

seriously. "I've known that from day one."

Problem solved.

While the first few days of the trip home had been an absolute challenge it was easier after they got far enough north to get away from the continual hazards of crossing streams and rivers. They reached Missouri which was being surveyed about the same time as Arkansas. Missouri had a lot more trails that had been developed as people went farther west. Once they reached those areas they were able to use the wagons and made better progress.

They finally made it to the Mississippi River. Ethan asked the engineer where they were.

"I think we're somewhere above where the Ohio comes together with the Mississippi River." He continued to study the map. Based on what he knew about the damage caused by the earthquake of 1811, he knew they were above the swamp.

"We are somewhere along here," he said. He pointed at the map and at the bluff in the distance.

They had made a choice between two trails the day before, believing the one they took would come out at a landing spot on the banks of the Mississippi. The question, though: were they above it? Or were they below it?

Ethan stared at the water of the Mississippi. It wasn't as muddy as he remembered it being in Memphis. He decided they must be above the Ohio River because that was where a lot of mud was added to the Mississippi.

Once again he wondered whether they would get back to Wayne County…or when.

CHAPTER 5

They had gathered all of their equipment, mules, and goods being carried by hand. They stood on the bank staring at the river. It was over a mile wide, and no telling how deep the water was at the point where they stood.

Should we unpack and camp? Or retrace our steps yet again?

"What is that?" Noah yelled. He pointed upstream. Just coming into sight was something large. It quickly became obvious that it was a raft of logs rapidly coming directly towards them.

"Back up! Back up!" yelled the engineer. It looked as if the logs were going to come ashore. As they scrambled to get away, they heard people yelling from somewhere on the logs.

"Push! Push! We got to keep these logs in the river!"

When the yelling stopped there was a pile of logs hard against and on the bank. The survey crew had managed to get the mules under control, and realized just how lucky they were not to have been in the river when the logs came ashore.

The engineer and the logger in charge of the raft began talking.

"Could we hire you guys to help get the logs back into the river?" the logger asked.

Ethan turned to Noah. "Do you remember when logs would pass us on our way with Colonel Jackson?"

"Yes, I remember. They had camps on top of the logs."

Ehan went forward and waited for a chance to say something. "If we help you get back in the river, can we ride the raft to Memphis?" he interjected.

They struck a deal.

For the next two days the logs were repositioned and fastened together securely. All of the survey crew's equipment was distributed evenly long the middle of the raft. The raft was some 45 feet wide and over 450 feet long. The logging crew had a camp of sorts that was about 20 feet from the back of the logs. The perimeter logs had been fastened together, and were larger than any of the others.

The camp for the survey crew was rather elaborate. The wheels had been taken off the wagons, and with tents spread above each wagon bed they became separate rooms.

The atmosphere was festive as they began the float towards Memphis. The colored crew of nine men had been quickly been welcomed by the large, raw boned Scandinavian loggers. The loggers were strong and could change the direction of the raft using their poles. It only took the colored men a couple of miles to master the art of sticking the pole in the river gaining leverage against the edge to keep the raft in the direction it needed to go.

"If you men had'a been on board we would've never lost these logs into the river bank," the head logger commented.

"If you loggers had'a never crashed into the riverbank we would still be standing there trying to figure out how to get across," Ethan answered.

The logs were destined for a sawmill just south of the bluff at Memphis. Upon arrival the logs were gathered into a bayou created by the earthquake of 1811.

It took a day to unload and reassemble the wagons, and for the survey crew to come ashore. Ethan spent quite a while saying his goodbyes to each one of the colored men. Although they had started out as slaves in his mind, in three years they had become like brothers to him. It took him longer to say goodbye to one colored man in particular. During those three years Ethan had watched this friend not only learn the letters of the alphabet, but also learn to read and write.

Ethan walked slowly towards where Noah stood holding the reins of the mule, waiting for him so they could leave Memphis.

Their first stop was the bank of Memphis to see if the conscript given to them by the engineer could be cashed for three years' pay. Ethan read it twice. "Payable to Ethan Massey and Noah Sitton $960 each for three years work as survey assistants in Arkansas."

$1920.00 That was a fortune in October, 1819. And Ethan still had the conscript from his Army discharge. He only hoped, though, he had enough money after he got back to Wayne County to buy everything they would need for their trip back to Arkansas.

CHAPTER 6

Ethan watched Noah Sitton come up the trail toward the house where he sat relaxing on the porch. Noah seemed shorter than the 5'7" Ethan remembered him being when they had joined Colonel Jackson. There hadn't been much training when they joined the Tennessee Volunteers. The men were all skilled with rifles because they had grown up hunting to provide meat for food.

Ethan also observed that Noah seemed to have darker hair. He'd remembered it being a sandy light brown, not as dark as now. He wondered if he actually looked shorter than the 6' he measured when they joined the military. He remembered Noah joking, "We're being measured for the coffin if we get killed in New Orleans."

When they came home they had expected to return to Arkansas in a couple of months. When they made a trip to Memphis to get a copy of the new maps and the details of the survey, they had been told it would be a while.

It had now been two years.

Noah stepped up on the porch and sat down without saying a word.

"You look serious today," Ethan commented.

"I am," Noah replied as he reached forward and pushed Ethan's hound away from him. The dog was about four years old, and by his markings he was a mixed breed between a black and tan and the more traditional blue tick hound of Tennessee.

"Best dog in the county," said Ethan.

Noah couldn't argue with that, even though the litter mate he had seemed to just be lazy. There were four male pups in the litter, but their grandfather Bryant let a fur trader have two of them before they returned from Arkansas.

Noah held the dog's head after pushing him away. "You ever wonder about those other two pups?"

"I wonder about a lot of things," Ethan replied. "Like if we'll ever get together on who's going to Arkansas and who's staying here."

"Oh," Noah stretched his arms and yawned. "We'll get it figured out."

Ethan had grown tired of this conversation during the last two years. At first everybody seemed eager to go. Ethan had been really careful when answering everyone's questions.

"I don't want to give the wrong impression," he had said so many times. He wondered if he even knew what to say.

When he described all the good things, like how great the timber was with an unlimited forest, how the woods were full of game with deer for meat and all kinds of furbearing animals to trap, it sounded like a land where you would never have to work. But when he talked about the rocks, saw briars, hornets, horse flies, not to mention snakes, it sounded almost intolerable.

The hard part was planning a journey with wagons and families; it had been almost impossible for a group of men with pack animals and supplies to make the trip.

"I'm going back." Ethan turned in his chair and faced Noah. "I'm leaving next spring. The only question is who is going with me?"

His thoughts turned to the youngest of the Blair daughters just over the ridge. He had gone to see her but had not asked for her hand in marriage. He tried to paint a picture of what their lives could be like in that place on top of a flat in Arkansas. He described the rolling prairie sitting on top of the hills surrounding the area.

"If Mama and Daddy goes---," she replied.

Ethan didn't know how to give an answer that was not his to provide. He had never attempted to talk the Blair family into making the move because of his fear of all the problems they would encounter with the trip and finding the right place to settle.

Since returning to Tennessee he heard horror stories from people who tried to move across the Mississippi River. Some talked about losing everything while trying to get through the swamp. Others mentioned not having any accurate maps, no place to get supplies, and having to wait for the fur traders to return with the orders they had taken when they left to pick up furs.

It had not improved from what Ethan could tell from the stories.

Noah and I know more about how to do this than any of those people who just left on their own without having any idea what they were doing.

"Noah, if we leave in March before the spring rains and thaw, do you think we could cross the Mississippi around Memphis?"

"I have discussed all of this with my folks," Noah answered. "We don't want to be like those folks that left last year and gave everything they had to their neighbors. Then they got to Memphis and couldn't cross the river. Came back with wagons that really weren't in good enough shape to leave in the first place. The wagons fell apart a few miles before they got back."

Ethan sat up straight, took the dog's head in his hands and said, "We will be better prepared."

He remembered the two neighbors Noah had mentioned. They were definitely now lifetime enemies. After the one family returned home, they kicked their neighbors out of the house they had given them for the rest of their lives. They also took back all of the animals they had given them.

All of these people had either been friends or enemies as long as Noah could remember. He thought about all the things he had learned about his own family, the Massey clan, and all the moves they had made since they landed on the eastern shore of what was now the United States. They, along with the same group of people that now lived in Wayne County, had continuously moved west when more settlers arrived. There were friendships that went all the way back to the old country, and there were enemies that went back there, also.

They always dreamed of being able to move with only those that got along really well to make up the new community. But there were marriages and friendships that always seemed to bring along the whole group.

"I am going to talk to all of my family, and those that want to go can go, and those that don't can stay here," Ethan said as he stroked the dog's head. "My girl and my dog are going with me."

Ethan stood up and Noah followed him to the barn. They looked at the wagon and all the work that had been done to prepare it for the trip. The wheels were in perfect shape. The wagon bed had been extended to accommodate a covering, and the bows for the canvas lay inside the bed waiting to be attached.

"Do you think one team of mules can pull the wagon?" Noah asked. He had acquired a number of pack mules and equipment to be carried by the mules.

"I've got four good pack mules and two huge mules that can pull this wagon," Ethan answered.

They returned to the porch and watched as the sun sank lower in the west.

Noah planned to go north across the Ohio River into Illinois and cross the Mississippi into Missouri somewhere above where they caught the raft of logs coming home. He told Ethan several times of his plan. Ethan listened each time, but never agreed. Somebody would have to make the decision.

CHAPTER 7

Ethan sat on the wagon seat staring at the Ohio River before him. Sarah Blair was now Sarah Massey. They were married over a month before they loaded the wagon and began their journey to Arkansas. His dog lay resting below the seat.

"Is this the crossing?" Ethan asked as Noah led one of his pack mules up to where they had stopped.

"I hope so," Noah replied. He turned to look at the string of wagons coming to a stop.

Nine wagons were left from the group who had left Wayne County. Ethan and Noah argued whether they had lost three or five. Definitely close to one fourth of their party had turned around and gone back to Wayne County. For some this was their second return.

"Do you think the Stennet's will get their house back again?" Noah asked. His mouth turned up on one side in a half smile as he visualized the fight that surely had ensued because it was the second time they had given the homestead away and would now want it back again.

Noah looked at the situation at hand. They had crossed several smaller streams in the twenty-one days since leaving Wayne County. But now it looked almost like the spot on the Mississippi where they had caught the log raft to Memphis. The scouts had gone ahead, trying to make sure they were on the right route, and they had not returned for the day.

"Jacob and Ed should've been back by now. This just doesn't look right," Ethan commented. Then they saw Jacob and Ed coming toward them.

"They have moved the tether cable," Jacob said, pointing up the river.

"There was a washout and it became impossible to cross here," Ed added.

Ethan had heard about the tether line for crossing the Ohio. It was similar to what the colored men did to make it possible for them to cross the Buffalo River on their way back from the survey. The tether line was a cable stretched a couple of feet above the water and secured on each shore. There were ropes attached to rings that would slide along the cable after being tied to the wagons to prevent them from being washed downstream.

There were a couple of ferry boats, but trying to load and then unload to use them did not appeal to either Ethan or Noah.

While planning for the trip they had visited at length with one of the fur buyers about the tether line system. They decided it made more sense and would be a lot quicker than loading and unloading a ferry, and the cost was practically nothing to pay the three men operating the tether.

Noah looked at the sun. "It will be sundown before long."

"We just as well make camp," said Ethan.

The slowest part of the journey had been stopping for

camp and breaking camp every morning to leave.

"I just wish I knew how much time we spent making camp," Noah mused as he decided how to create the camp they needed for the night. Since the beginning of traveling by wagon trains all camps were made by creating a circle of wagons, both for safety and for socializing.

Ethan drove his wagon to the spot he thought would be the starting point for the next morning. The other wagons then formed the circle, just like all the other stops they had made. Then the children, who had been forced to sit quietly behind the wagon seat during the day, came out and began to play within the circle of wagons.

Noah watched the children, thinking that it wouldn't be long until the spot for tonight's campfire would be trampled down clean enough to set out the cooking utensils and get ready for preparing tonight's meal.

Ethan was restless and worried. "Sarah, this is the part I've been dreading. We have two big rivers to cross. I still wish I could've talked Noah into going to the crossing above Memphis."

Sarah had heard this many times before. She remembered the discussions for the last two months about the cost loading all of the wagons, animals, and people onto a barge that was very undependable, not counting that one group had been lost in the middle of the river. Noah would not agree to spend the money for that, and his group of followers had voted to take the route north into Illinois and cross the shoals of the Mississippi River below St. Louis.

Ethan became quiet as he unhitched the team of mules from the wagon. He thought about how helpful Noah was by allowing him to use any number of the pack mules to help pull the wagon through any area when he needed help. Maybe this was the right way to do it.

"We will find out tomorrow," he said as he looked up the trail that Jacob and Ed had come down a little while before. There was a crossing in place a couple of hours upstream.

The crossing had gone a lot better than expected. There had even been some excitement.

Ethan and Sarah sat safely on the Illinois side of the Ohio River watching as the other wagons came across to join them.

Sarah jumped to her feet yelling, "Oh my God, it's mother!"

Ethan jumped from the wagon and ran back toward the river, trying to figure out what was going on. Two boys from behind the Blair wagon appeared to be chasing something floating down the river.

"Get it! Get it!! Get it!!!" yelled Mrs. Blair. It was a crate that contained four hens. Mrs. Blair had insisted she be able to bring twelve hens. "They are my four best ones!"

They watched as the crate floated out of sight but appearing as if it might come ashore on their side of the river.

After everyone was safely across, which had taken most of the day, Noah suggested they might be able to recover the chickens if they drifted ashore. But Ethan did not want to camp close to the river. He was sure their camp would be disturbed by more people coming to cross the river. And they did not want to get mixed in with another party. Their group were settling in and were able to work together and he didn't want to take a chance of having that interrupted.

Ethan and Noah discussed the folks in the wagons who gave up up and returned to Wayne County. Ethan didn't even consider the two modified buggies as being wagons. He didn't have a name for the contraptions the Baker family had assembled to make the trip. He just knew that three days out they were not able to keep up with the rest of the wagons. They gave up and returned with the two carts. Three other wagons with Noah's cousins turned back because they had forgotten to bring enough supplies.

Ethan had loaned his cousin Jeff $30 to buy supplies

before starting the trip. When they stopped at a trading post just before they got out of Tennessee Jeff began picking up supplies. Then he said, "Ethan, I need $26 more."

Ethan was shocked. He didn't say a word. He walked out and climbed onto his wagon. When he looked back, Jeff and two other cousins turned around and headed back to Wayne County.

The wagon road west was well traveled on this side of the river and they made good time until they stopped at an open area high enough away from the river to make a good camp. Ethan signaled the wagons they were stopping for the night.

Soon two colored boys came directly up the riverbank carrying the crate of chickens that had been lost while they were crossing the river. One appeared to be about 12 or 14, the other one at least three years younger. They set the crate down at the Blairs wagon.

"Ma'am, we watched you lose this, and we chased it ever so far. We even lost our fishing poles when we were trying to get it out of the river."

The hens sat contentedly inside. They actually looked better than they did before the crate went in the river. The hens had survived the bath rather well, and the crate was nice and clean.

Sarah hugged her mother, and Ethan and Mr. Blair placed the crate back in the wagon. Mrs. Blair rewarded the boys with Johnny cakes as they turned to return to the river.

Ethan's thoughts returned to Memphis when he held the hand of the colored friend he made during the survey. He remembered how hesitant he was to make the friendship because of the things he had been taught about their ability to learn. He had always assumed that slaves were slaves because that was all they were capable of doing. Ross, as he learned to call his colored friend, was unbelievably smart. He had also shown character.

Ethan watched the two young men returning to the river.

They had shown the same character as Ross.

"Ethan, can you believe that?' Sarah asked as she caught up with him. "Mother is thrilled to death. She made sure daddy tied that crate on all four corners. She ain't takin' any more chances on losing them hens."

They were relieved to be across the Ohio and on a well-traveled wagon trail. The people from Wayne County only hoped when they broke camp tomorrow it would be the right trail to arrive at a good crossing when they got to the Mississippi.

CHAPTER 8

"Sarah, I kinda like this along here," Ethan said as the wagon rolled smoothly along the well-worn trail.

"Better than Arkansas?"

"Nah," grunted Ethan. He watched his dog running just outside the trail, sniffing several spots as he passed over them. He had never attempted to get far enough away for Ethan to have to stop and bring him back. Just yelling "Chase" was enough.

"Sarah I had trouble deciding on that dog's name," Ethan explained. "Until one night me and Noah was following the dogs as they chased something across the valley below the farm." When I realized how far in front he was, I turned to Noah and said, "Your dogs are not even in the chase."

"Not my fault they can't keep up the chase."

"I thought he said they can't keep up with Chase," Noah said.

Sarah wondered how Ethan had ignored her question

about comparing where they were to Arkansas, and instead began talking about his dog. She knew he had been proud of the dog when he got the pup. She remembered him complaining that he wanted a traditional blue tick hound like everybody else. He wondered where the black and tan blood had come from because there was no one close to him with any black and tan hounds. He fell in love with the dog and was so proud when Noah's pup from the same litter was not able to keep up with Chase.

"This don't compare with Arkansas," Ethan finally said.

"What's different?" Sarah asked. She looked to the north at the broken ridges of low mountains that seemed to be just above the level plain they were traveling across.

Ethan looked at the scrub brush and willows growing along the north side of the Ohio River. He looked at the mixture of grasses along the trail. He looked at the timber to the north, not sure if it was scrub oak or other hardwoods, mixed with an undergrowth that choked out any grass. Then he tried to visualize the different terrains he had seen in Arkansas.

"Sarah, it's not possible for me to describe where we're headed in Arkansas. But we are not going anywhere near those swamps with all the snakes and mosquitoes. We are headed back to the place where we were on a mountain top. Big Flat."

He remembered several times during the survey when they left Big Flat going south they came to a different formation of rocks. The mountains were bigger and there were more big boulders than the flat sandstones. When they went north down the creeks from big flat there was bench land above the bluffs with bottomland along the creeks. Any time they climbed back up through the hollows to return to big flat there would be another level of land.

"I know you will like Arkansas, Sarah." Ethan turned to check the wagons to see if they were all moving together. "The air will not be sticky like it is here and in Tennessee.

It's covered with large oak trees, not any of the scrub brush thickets along here." He pointed at the scrub brush on their right where Chase had disappeared trying to sniff out the trail of some animal. Ethan didn't worry about the dog wandering off. After five weeks on the trail he'd come to trust Chase to stay with the wagon.

"Who will build our house?" Sarah asked.

Ethan had tried to explain before they got married that he and Noah would exchange work and build their houses together. After Sarah's parents had agreed to come along with them, it added extra work for more homes, but Ethan was convinced Sarah's dad would be great help. He had the best cabin in Wayne County, Tennessee, and he had built it with his two brothers in a very short period of time. One of those brothers was in a wagon immediately behind Sarah's folks.

Ethan did not bothered to count people or animals before the wagons would move out after camp. They had agreed in the beginning that each wagon driver would signal when they were ready to travel, meaning all was well and they were ready to go.

So, it was disturbing when they discovered they were missing one of Sarah's cousins, a young lady just younger than Sarah, and one of Noah's cousins, a young man just younger than Ethan.

"I thought they were going to get married after we got to Arkansas," Sarah said when they discovered them gone the morning after they crossed the Ohio River.

"Jeb never said a word to me, had no idea he was going to pull this stunt," commented Noah.

Their timing had been perfect.

"I bet they left while we were crossing the river with all the excitement of keeping everything together," Sarah said.

"Yeah, and they knew we were not going to cross back to look for them," Noah added.

Everyone worried how they were going to find their way

back, or how they were going to exist wherever they were.

"I'll bet they've got a plan," Ethan concluded.

How much farther it was before they would catch the ferry across the Mississippi was a mystery. Noah and Ethan thought it would probably take 10 or 12 days from the Ohio River to the ferry.

They had traveled a little over a week when they encountered a fur trader heading east. Ethan asked if they were on the right road to the ferry across the Mississippi.

"There's four camps full of wagons waiting their turn to ride the ferry," had been the answer.

"Why?"

"It's the slowest thing you have ever seen in your life," the fur trader answered. "It didn't take me long to catch the ferry back across because I was coming east." He turned and pointed west. "When you're going that way it's crowded, and the river's hard to cross, trying to time it to where the ferry doesn't get hit by a raft of logs."

Ethan shuddered. He remembered how they had almost gotten wiped out by logs coming ashore. He could only imagine Sarah and his dog in a wagon on the ferry and a raft of logs colliding with the ferry.

"What do you think about all that, Noah?"

They watched the fur trader and his pack mules pass out of sight heading east.

"We've dealt with worse," Noah answered.

Ethan recalled the three days it took to ferry the survey crew with everything they needed across, and then the trouble they had in the swamps of Arkansas. There was no way it could be that bad crossing the Mississippi to Missouri.

It had been four days since they talked to the trapper, and the travel had been easy compared to coming north out of Tennessee and crossing Kentucky. The road was more traveled and there was good water and good campsites.

Sarah stood up. "I believe I see wagons," she said.

"I've been hearing dogs barking for a while," Ethan said.

Chase had not stirred from underneath the wagon seat during all the commotion. Ethan wondered if his dog was tired from his morning run or if he was sick. He wondered why Chase wasn't up barking back at the dogs that were obviously from the wagons camped ahead.

But none of the other dogs in the rest of the wagons had made a sound, either. Maybe they were just trail weary.

Ethan pulled the wagons off into a spot that had obviously been a camp a few nights before. There was the usual circle, the center dominated by what had been a campfire.

"I guess this is where we wait for our turn to move forward to get on the ferry," Ethan told everyone as they came to a stop. No one was happy with the idea of having to camp and wait your turn for the ferry.

CHAPTER 9

Ethan sat looking back at the Mississippi. He was so proud when he counted the wagons and everybody reported they were safe and sound.

It had been really hard to be patient while they camped waiting their turn to be ferried across the river. Noah had become irritable and griped when he found out how much it was going to cost for the ferry. He realized that of the wagons they had three without enough money to pay for crossing the river.

"Ethan, do you know I've spent almost half of my money that I planned to make it to Arkansas with," Noah said.

Ethan thought about the money belt he bought after they got home. He bought it after his hiding places was discovered and someone borrowed money. It happened while he was trying to convince every Massey relative to accompany him back to Arkansas, but it seemed they only understood the bad parts.

"Noah, I know you and I are bankrolling this journey to Arkansas because our families who have money and are doing well in Wayne County didn't see a reason to pick up and leave."

He turned and looked at all the wagons following them. They left Wayne County because they thought they could do better in Arkansas. It didn't matter what their names were.

"We know there is opportunity in Arkansas," Ethan continued. "Our families have the best farms in Wayne County, Tennessee. I don't know why we ever thought they would just uproot and leave because we fell in love with the land we helped survey."

They walked together back toward the Mississippi River they had just crossed. Ethan's eyes grew misty as he stared back toward the other side. He had no idea how far Wayne County was or how long it would be if he ever saw it again, now that he was married to Sarah and the Blair families were moving with them.

Noah Sitton had a wagon full of supplies, some of it belonging to his family with instructions. "Noah, you go find the best land possible, come back, and we'll all move with you," his father, Nathaniel had said as he gave tools and things he could spare for Noah to take with him.

It was too late for regrets.

"We've done it now," Noah said. They turned and walked back to their wagons. "We're over halfway there," he said as they got back to the wagons to settle in for another night of camping.

As Ethan tried to sleep, he recalled how much easier it had been to cross the river using the ferry boats that were built for crossing. He liked the rope corrals on the upper side of the ferry used to control the livestock people took with them. He had visited with people heading everywhere. Some planned to settle in western Missouri, some farther along the streams that flowed into the Mississippi. And the money they spent for the ferry didn't seem as expensive when you considered the ferry operator had a crew to help manage all of the people, wagons, and supplies that went with each group.

Ethan finally went to sleep. It was too late to question his decision. Noah had delayed their departure for almost a year, hoping that a Wallace girl would become his wife and be sitting beside him on the wagon seat just like Sarah was with Ethan.

For two guys that had hoped to be moving a huge part of their families with them, they were absolute failures.

Ethan dreamed of sending back money from all the furs he could trap in two years, and bring every cousin he had to live by him in Arkansas.

He was awake and climbed from the wagon. It was the end of May, 1823, and he was proud it was a beautiful morning, and he was definitely on his way to Arkansas.

The wagons pulled out onto the trail. Noah had purchased a map the ferryman assured him was accurate and would take them to a place just north of White River in Arkansas. He studied the map trying to pinpoint where they were located.

They had come to a river. The problem was there was no designation for the river or the ferry. They were going to have to get across somehow.

After they finally made it across, Noah was not sure how long the ferry had been there. It was nothing more than a raft made from logs. The bigger logs were fastened together and then smaller trees were used to fill in spaces between them to create a floor. It had been hard to convince everybody it was safe, there were canoes around the edge to transport the people and keep the raft moving in the right direction.

Noah would not forget when half the wagons were on the other side of the river, the ferry Captain said, "This is a lot more trouble than I thought it was going to be." And he increased the price by fifty percent.

"I don't know of anything we can do about it," Ethan said. "We can't leave half the people on the other side and split up. We have to get across and go on to Arkansas."

Noah had agreed, but he was not happy that they'd had no choice but to pay the increased fee. "This doesn't compare to how nice the people were when we caught the raft coming back from Arkansas," he said.

The hills of Missouri were becoming bigger, and the mules pulling the wagons were not making nearly the progress they had hoped for. The sun began to set on their fourth day of travel after crossing the Mississippi.

Ethan looked for another campsite. They had been assured that this was a well-traveled trail, but since they had left the last river they had only met two fur traders with five or six pack mules apiece. The ruts of the trail were dried hard. It looked like the last wagon train had gone through after a rain and made the deep ruts. Ethan did not believe it had rained in over a week. He did not point this out to Noah. Noah was still disgusted.

It was the second day of travel since leaving the river not indicated on the map. The camp sites had been good ones next to clear streams of water, and there had been plenty of forage for all of their animals. Progress may have been slow, but at least they hadn't run into any problems.

Staring down the trail trying to make sure that they were still following the markers on the map kept Ethan's mind occupied. He wasn't looking ahead of the wagon, and was almost in shouting distance before he realized they had caught up with another group of travelers.

Ethan recognized Nathan Campbell standing in the middle of the trail. Nathan was the father of Jim Campbell who had disappeared from the survey crew. As the wagons pulled closer Nathan stepped aside and asked, "Where did you guys come from?"

After the shock of recognition, questions began to flow.

Noah jumped down from his wagon and ran to join them.

"When we left Tennessee, Nathan, you guys were still trying to decide if you were going to make the trip," said Noah. "And now I'm looking at your wagon sitting in the trail in front of ours!" He looked at them in disbelief. "How?"

Nathan Campbell leaned against the side of Ethan's wagon.

"We left three days after you did." He stepped forward and looked back down the trail. "We made it to the Mississippi and to the first crossing above Memphis in less than a week. A barge was having to wait for logs to clear, and became a ferry for two or three days and we made it across the river with no problems. We followed the trail along the east side of the ridges and didn't lose any time in the swamp."

Ethan's dog made several circles among all the wagons now stopped on the trail.

"He recognizes a lot of these pups that are here because we hunted together back in Wayne County," Ethan said.

"Earl is the reason we're stopped," Nathan abruptly said.

"Earl?" asked Ethan.

"Yes. Your dad. His is the wagon all the way in the front. Your mom is not feeling well."

Ethan broke into a run, dodging between wagons to miss the dogs and people until he made it to his where his mom and dad sat beside their wagon. They were looking at a broken axle and a skid pole lying on the ground behind the wagon.

There had never been a more heartfelt greeting than when Ethan realized he was no longer making the trip to Arkansas alone. There would be Masseys, lots of them, once they got to Big Flat.

CHAPTER 10

It had been a festive evening after they finished the repairs on Earl Massey's wagon. They pulled off in a circle as usual to make camp, only this time Ethan led the wagons as they took their places to make camp. Ethan counted 17 wagons, with Noah Sitton still following immediately behind him, then Sarah's parents with two of her uncles immediately behind them.

"Pap, are you going to lead us tomorrow?" Ethan asked, wondering what the proceedings were going to be now that they were all together.

"Nope," Earl answered. "Me and your ma are going to the back of the line." He paused. "We'll make sure everybody keeps up, and that we don't lose anybody along the trail."

Ethan walked toward Noah as he came to join them.

"Will you look at that map some more, Noah, before it gets dark?"

Noah turned back toward his wagon. "Come on," he

answered over his shoulder, "we'll try to figure it out."

They unrolled the map and spread it against the side of the wagon using the two holes in the upper corners to hang it in place. Ethan just then realized the map was on a piece of deerskin that had been hand cleaned as you would prepare a hide for making a coat or deerskin shirt. The markings had been burned in with a sharp instrument. The wider jagged lines represented streams, and the straight, narrow lines were trails between the streams.

While they had looked at the map before, they'd usually unrolled it on the ground, and only tried to figure out where they were and where they were going next. Now they saw it differently, as a plan for not only a day's travel but to make sure they arrived in the proper spot to cross into Arkansas. As they stepped back farther from the wagon to study the entire map, Ethan recognized the same features that had been on the engineer's map when they were surveying. The one straight line that went across the entire map just below its midsection was the Mason-Dixon line between Arkansas territory and Missouri territory.

"Noah, this map is no better than the one that kept us lost for over three years," Ethan said disgustedly as he spat and walked away.

Noah followed him. "I am proud none of the others are taking the time to look at this with us." He let out a deep breath. He looked up at Ethan, realizing for the first time that his partner of over six years had grown a couple of inches.

They walked back to the map and placed their fingers on the spot where they thought they were standing. They looked at the distance left to travel to Arkansas. It was greater than the distance they had already come since crossing the Mississippi River.

The markings were a combination of trails that followed the eastern side of streams going south to a spot where a note marked a crossing. Then they would journey straight west until time to do the same thing, again following the streams south until it was time to cross again.

"Ethan, you think we would've been better off going up to St. Louis and joining one of the wagon trains heading to the prairie?" Noah asked.

"No!" Ethan replied. "I know what I want; a place where I can see for some good distance, a place with big oak trees, a place with grassland and cedar glades, with a mixture of sycamore and willows along the streams full of fish and big rocks. No swamps, no mosquitos, very few snakes."

Noah agreed, then walked toward his wagon, leaving Ethan to figure out where they were going to go.

It was easier than Ethan expected to break camp and get on the trail with all of the additional wagons that were now part of their party. The mood was good as families tried to catch up on stories and to figure out where they were going.

The sun was getting higher in the sky every day as they started their travels, it was late spring, almost summer, and with the longer days they should be able to travel farther every day.

It had been six days since the parties had joined together. There had been very few problems. Ethan felt better knowing his parents were with him. He and his dad exchanged waves each time they were ready to go, and again when they stopped. The full length of the wagons on the trail stretched for over a mile with all the animals, and all the dogs following along. Most of the time the people walked behind the wagons, and only rode in the wagons when they became tired. By having everyone stay out of the wagons, it was less load for the mules to pull, and the wagons would last longer by carrying less weight.

The biggest concern was the amount of supplies they had versus the amount they were going to need before they got settled and able to make next year's crops. Earl Massey, Noah, and Ethan asked each family to give an account of how much food they had with them. Earl spent the next two days trying to figure out their rations and the time it would take to get to Arkansas and produce food.

They began living off the land as much as they could. They feasted on the game they killed and the fish they caught. "We've only used ammunition and salt the last three days," Earl said.

Ethan wondered if there was any way they would know for sure when they crossed into Arkansas. Then he remembered the engineer saying the trees marking the boundary between Missouri and Arkansas would be blazed on all four sides six feet above the ground.

Three days later they saw trees with huge marks all around them. They had reached Arkansas. Now to reach their destination in Arkansas.

"Ethan, is this where we're living?" Sarah asked as Ethan jumped down from the wagon and ran toward the trees. Chase jumped down from the wagon, also, to see what the excitement was, and stopped when Ethan did.

Noah joined Ethan. They looked back to the east and then again to the west. "This is it," he said. The trail cut through a gap along the ridge just east of the river they had been following. The bushes, which had been trimmed to make the survey for the Mason-Dixon Line, had begun to grow back, but it was still obvious from the markings that they were now in Arkansas.

Noah went back to the wagon and retrieved the map from underneath his wagon seat. As they hung the map on the side of the wagon, a crowd gathered.

"Why are we stopped?" Sarah's dad, Newton Blair, asked.

Sarah went to his side, smiling. "We're in Arkansas," she said.

"This is it?" Her dad looked around at all the scrub bushes along the rocky ridge.

"We are nowhere close to where we're going," Ethan said.

"How much farther is it?" asked one of the children whose task was to lead a milch cow.

Noah spoke up. "Depends on where we go."

"We've come all this way, crossed all these rivers, wore ourselves out packing and unpacking while we camped, and we get here to Arkansas and we don't know where we're going?" commented one of Noah's cousins. "My wife's pop has been in Arkansas for almost three years. Trouble is, I don't know where I am, and I don't know where he is." He laughed, breaking the sour mood of the crowd.

"My daddy used to tell the same kind of stories about when they came through the gap and made it to Wayne County," added Ethan's mother after the laughter stopped.

Everyone returned to their wagons and they continued their journey.

Three days of travel in Arkansas had gone rather well. They continued to add to their stock of supplies by drying deer jerky hung from wires strung along the side of the wagons. Ethan had told them too keep the meat hanging in the sun. "It's the only way it will dry and not spoil," he said.

They arrived at a large camp with a lot of wagons, a lot of people, and several log shacks which appeared to have been built for temporary shelter.

A tall, slender fellow with big hand showing signs of hard work, and sharp, blue eyes introduced himself as Jake McCoy. "Old Joe stopped at this spot and stayed almost two years," he said.

"Do you live here?" Ethan asked.

"Nah, I live across the river and up the mountain," McCoy answered.

"What are you doing here now?"

"I come to meet some wagons that should've been here a month ago."

"From where?" asked Ethan.

"Just west of Nashville in Tennessee. They are my wife's folks, a bunch of folks named Treat," Jake turned and walked back toward where he was camped.

Noah and Ethan followed him, more curious than ever about where the guy had come from, and who the people were he was meeting. They remembered hearing stories of McCoys in eastern Tennessee. They were not sure they had ever heard the name Treat before.

During the time they had waited and planned their trip back to Arkansas, they knew people from all over had gone to Arkansas as soon as they heard it had been approved as a territory after the survey was completed in 1819. They didn't realize how many people had made it there during the time they had tried to get organized.

Ethan's thoughts were obviously on his face when Jake McCoy turned around and faced them again.

"We don't mean to pry in your business, but we were here and did the survey," Noah said. "We didn't know that immediately there would be this many people trying to get to Arkansas." He paused, then walked closer towards Jake.

"I brought supplies by pack mules to all the survey crews as fast as I could make the trips from St. Louis to Arkansas," Jake said. "I know these hills probably better than anybody, because I had to search for the survey crews each time I came, and the only way I could find them was to follow the new cut paths they made as they did the survey."

Ethan's curiosity got the better of him. "You ever go up those mountains?" he asked, pointing to the south and west, across the river from where they stood.

"Yep." Jake walked to his horse and removed a tattered map from the saddlebag, and spread it on the ground. As they bent over to look at the map, Noah and Ethan realized it was a duplicate of the one they bought just after. They crossed the Mississippi. There were a bunch of newer markings added to McCoy's map.

"If you go through here," Jake said, pointing to two trails that led south and west from where they were, then he stood and pointed across the river, "you will go through where all the Cherokees have been camped for years." He bent back over the map and pointed to a trail that went north of the river several miles before it turned south and followed one of the streams.

"If you go this first trail, you will have to go up the mountain." Jake stood again and pointed toward the highest mountain on the southern horizon. "That sucker's steep. You have to unload your wagons and make probably three trips, because your mules can barely pull the wagons up that thing. There's a lot of wagons that have run off the side of the mountain after stalling out." He looked at their wagons. "We have nicknamed it "Push Mountain" because the only people that have made it over it are the ones that were strong enough to literally push their wagons and help their mules make it to the top."

Ethan's dad had joined them and had been listening to the last parts of the conversation. He was positive that he was not going to lose a wagon or mules after being told how hard the trip would be.

"We're not going that way!" he declared.

After making plans to leave in the morning and go west until they could go up the stream and across the river, they settled down for the night.

CHAPTER 11

"**I** don't really remember ever seeing that McCoy fellow," Noah said. They had stopped the wagons for their first break after heading up the river to cross where the stream came in from the south.

"We was always gone when the supplies came to camp," Ethan replied. "I remember seeing them come into camp a couple times as we were leaving to go back to survey."

Noah chewed on a piece of straw he had picked up beside the trail. He turned to answer Ethan. "I just don't remember ever seeing them." He paused. "Course I know he came, because we was there three years and never ran out of supplies."

Ethan wondered how many more people knew about Arkansas. They had worked their way through a bunch of camps after they had left the place everyone called "Old Joe." Ethan thought it was a weird name for a place. Why would you name a place Old Joe? He continued thinking. They just couldn't cross the river, work their way through a bunch of camps, and climb a mountain to arrive at Big Flat if the Wallaces had already established a trading post by the spring.

Ethan's dream would have to be adjusted. He was not going to try to explain to Sarah that all the things he had described about being in a wide-open flat area with unlimited grass and a little round mountain on the horizon that would always mark the spot they were going to call home wasn't possible.

He reached down and stroked Chase's head as he tried to imagine their new home would have to be somewhere along the creeks after they crossed the White River. He wondered how the White River got its name. He had now learned three names: Push Mountain, Old Joe, and White River. He wasn't counting Big Flat yet. Chase gave out a yawn as if to say, "Who cares?" Ethan finished stroking the dog's head.

The wagons traveled through an area that was rough to ride. The limestone outcroppings continuously jolted the wagons, making it hard for the mules to pull the wagons up and over. When they started down the grades after crossing one of the little ridges, the limestone ledges had the opposite effect of causing the wagons to lurch forward and push the mules down the grade.

This terrain lasted for most of the day. It ended after they crossed the North Fork of the White River and began to climb a hill above the river. They. Made camp in a cedar glade.

Noah walked slowly to the spot where Ethan had stopped his wagon. "Do you remember enough about the land along the creeks west of Big Flat to know where we're going?" he asked.

Ethan realized while they'd been back in Tennessee, all the streams had been given names. "After we head up the Buffalo River, we'll turn up the Big Creek by where we had to go around that swirl. Remember that?"

"Yeah, I remember that," Noah answered. "I also remember we couldn't cross the river where Big Creek ran in to the Buffalo." They used the two names they had heard while camped at Old Joe.

"We'll figure it out when we get there," Ethan answered.

It had been almost three weeks since they had broken camp at Old Joe and decided to go up and cross White River, then travel up the Buffalo River until they came to Big Creek.

It had been easy to cross the Buffalo because the river had changed and split into two streams with a sandy island in the middle, and it was shallow on the upper end above where Big Creek joined the Buffalo River.

They made camp in a field someone had cleared where the two streams joined. Ethan tried to remember how many days they had been on the trail since leaving Wayne County, Tennessee. He broke the trip into segments. The first one was from Wayne County to the Ohio River. The second one was across Illinois to where they crossed the Mississippi. The third one was from the Mississippi until they reached Arkansas. And now they were traveling the fourth segment, along the streams trying to adjust their plans to not go to Big Flat.

Travel was easy along the creek. It was shallow enough to cross and the banks showed signs of wagons making the same crossing. This worried Ethan. When they were doing the survey, he's always thought he would have picking choice of the land when they returned. Now they were in Arkansas, and so were a lot of other folks.

The women were worn out from all the days of travel. Ethan knew they had been traveling over three months. He asked his dad what the day of the month it was.

"Son, it's June 26, 1823," Earl Massey said. "You all left about March 1st, and we left Wayne County March 10th," he added.

"Three and a half months to make it to a field planted in

corn. We don't know the owner, and we don't know where we're going, but we're going to get there too late to plant anything," Ethan whispered under his breath as he walked back to his wagon.

The search for happiness, the search for that perfect spot, the dream of having your own piece of land all weighed heavy on the minds of these people traveling together from Wayne County, Tennessee.

Ethan and Noah decided to go alone and try to find a place to settle. They left the camp. They went through a narrow little hollow where a stream flowed in to the Long Creek before it flowed into the upper part of the Big Creek they had followed since leaving the Buffalo River. Ethan rode Earl's horse, the best animal in camp.

They rode for at least a couple of miles following a well traveled wagon trail. They noticed the hollow was getting wider.

"Noah, I think this is valley we have been looking for," Ethan commented just as they crossed the little stream again.

They both looked up just in time to see four children running in front of them. They rode the horses faster and began to catch up to the children. There was a boy probably four years old, and a girl about the same age. They were followed by another little boy and girl a couple of years younger.

The children, terrified, screamed and ran faster.

"We gotta slow down, we're scarin' those kids to death," said Noah.

They stopped and sat quietly on their horses for a minute.

"Did you notice anything about those kids?" Ethan asked.

Noah stared up the trail where the children had disappeared. They heard dogs barking not far in the distance.

"Yes, I did," Noah answered. "Two of those kids were part colored. The other two were part Indian, and to tell the truth, that biggest boy looks like Jim Campbell."

Ethan's mind raced. He tried to remember how long it had been since Jim Campbell and one of the colored guys had disappeared from the survey crew. As he added up the months he thought of the ages of the children.

Jim Campbell and one of the colored slaves had worked together to chop brush in front of the survey crew. They always worked late and got up early ahead of the crew to start the next morning. One day they didn't return to camp. The crew had gone out the next morning to pick up the survey, and when they got to the end of the area that had been cleared, there were no tools and no men. They had just disappeared.

Ethan and Noah rode toward the sound of the dogs, anxious to see what they could learn. They saw the four children disappear between two cabins built parallel to a small bluff extending above the roofs of the cabins. The cabins were joined by a roof which connected the two of them just above the level of the front doors. They each appeared to be about ten paces long and four paces wide, huge for a cabin.

Noah stopped a few paces behind Ethan and started to dismount. Ethan turned.

"I don't believe we should do that yet," he said as he motioned for Noah to stay mounted. They heard someone blow a Fox horn, three short blasts, from somewhere above the cabins.

Noah remounted and rode up beside Ethan. They sat quietly observing the surroundings above and below the two cabins in front of them. There were cleared areas with little patches of growing vegetables. There were a number of trees which had poles stretched between them, obviously for hanging game while the hides were skinned. The roofs of the cabins were split wood shingles perfectly aligned, in keeping with the skills that Jim Campbell's families had possessed for years.

"It's definitely Jim's," said Ethan.

They saw two pack mules coming toward the cabins.

Ethan watched the man coming toward them. He did not recognize his old friend until he was within a few paces of them. He definitely looked older than the boy who had joined the survey crew when they were in Memphis.

"Well, I'll be." Jim Campbell stopped and stared. "It's you, Ethan!" He walked toward his old friend. "Been expecting you, but gave up after a couple of years." Jim smiled, not a welcoming smile, but one that showed curiosity more than anything else.

"We been tryin' to get back for a while."

Noah still sat quietly on his horse, listening to Jim until he was sure he recognized the man who had the voice of the boy he remembered. He couldn't believe how much more broad-shouldered Jim had become. He was now at least six feet one, and had hair longer and blacker than he remembered. Jim was dressed in a pair of dungarees that probably came from St. Louis when the fur buyer came through. His shirt was one of the finest deerskin garments Noah had ever seen.

"Noah, get down from your horse and say something." Jim stepped toward him as if he was going to shake his hand, but gave him a hug instead. "It's so good to see you."

The colored man had stayed back some twenty feet from the three old friends, trying to make sense of who they were and how they got to this place. Jim turned to him.

"Come join us. You remember these guys."

Jim pointed to his colored friend. "This is Noel Milam."

"Zeke?" asked Ethan.

"Not anymore." Jim turned and walked to one of the cabins, leaving the three of them standing there. Ethan and Noah wondered why.

Jim returned, and without saying a word, handed a

leather pouch to Ethan. Inside was a piece of paper. Ethan studied the paper. It was a release of servitude issued to Noel Milam of the Milam plantation in Alabama. It stated that the "colored male, some 20 years old, is hereby released of all servitude and is considered a free man." It was dated and signed by "the owner of the above 20-year old colored slave."

Ethan handed the paper to Noah, then began asking Jim questions.

"How? Where? And who?" Ethan could not understand what this paper meant.

"You remember when we met the women," Jim Campbell began. He glanced toward the cabin for the first time. The children stood on the porches. An older boy and a younger girl were on one porch, and on the other porch it was the opposite, with an older girl and a younger boy. The women stood in the doorways of the cabins, watching the men some 30 paces away. And listening.

Jim continued, explaining they had a planned to leave the camp and come to this place with their girlfriends when they left the survey crew. The girls left their tribe and joined us in a search for a place to live.

"That still don't explain this piece of paper," interrupted Ethan as he handed the leather pouch containing the paper back to Jim.

"We got that," Jim answered, handing the pouch to Zeke. Who returned it to the cabin and placed above a post on the porch. "We were on our way to run the traps one morning," Jim continued, "and we came up on the fellow with those papers lying beside the trail with the back of his head blown away. We backed off quite a distance and sat watching the body. We hadn't gotten close enough to determine how long he may have been dead."

Ethan and Noah had gotten off their horses, led them to some trees, and now stood facing Jim as he told a very unbelievable story.

The summer heat was becoming almost unbearable, but there seemed to be a cool breeze underneath the trees where they stood. Ethan had noticed earlier how convenient the water was, coming out of the bluff immediately behind and below the cabins. The spring not only provided good, clean water, but the air circulating off of that water seemed to provide some coolness.

"After we sat and watched the body, Zeek asked why we hadn't smelled the guy," Jim said. "That caused me to wonder how close the killer might be."

Zeek had returned and now stood between Jim and Ethan.

"We decided to go closer and inspect the guy to see if we could figure out who he was and what had happened."

Jim turned and walked toward Ethan's horse. "Is that your dad, Earl's horse?" he asked. Before Ethan could answer, Jim went back to the story. He went on to tell how they had pulled the body onto the trail, while watching and listening in all directions for any sound of other people. He described how they had determined the dead colored man was about the same age they were.

"It was when we went through the vest he was wearing that we found the pouch with the paper," Jim said.

"I know I am here as legal as you guys," Jim went on, "but Zeke was a colored slave hired to help the survey." Jim took a step toward his friend, placing his hand on Zeek's shoulder. "Those papers gave him his freedom. That's who he is. We have roots now. We have wives and children." He spread his hands and turned in a circle, pointing in all directions. "We would have land if we knew where we were and had the survey notes where we could go to file the paperwork."

Noah spoke up for the first time. "I have all the field notes from the survey, along with the map of this area."

Jim's eyes lit up with excitement. "There's plenty of land in all directions in this valley for several families," he said, walking toward Noah. "How many families are with you guys?"

"Nineteen wagons," Ethan answered.

"Who?"

Ethan and Noah tried to name all the parties from Wayne County that were in the wagons, After the Blairs, Wallaces, and Masseys, the names kind of ran together. Noah waited for Jim's reaction.

"Noah, you didn't mention any Sittons or Rhodes families," Jim commented.

"That's because there ain't any of my family with us," Noah said. "I have tools and equipment to start building a homestead, but they're not coming until I say we have a good place to stay.

The women had been inching closer as the men conversed. Ethan had glanced at them as much as he could without being obvious. He noticed one, who he was sure was Jim's wife. She was exceptionally neat, with clean hair, and her clothes were well kept. They all wore shoes, including the children. The shoes had come from St. Louis. They told Ethan that trapping furs had been good business during the time he had been back in Tennessee. He looked further around the homesteads and he could see a lot of work had been done. The fenced areas for the animals were well built, and the sheds for pigs, chickens, and cows were well built also. But he did not see any animals.

"Where are your animals, Jim?" Ethan asked. He had only seen three mules.

"We have a fenced area above the bluff." Jim pointed above the cabins to an area that could not be seen from where they stood. "It's got a lot of good grass this time of year."

The conversation ended. Ethan and Noah turned and went to their horses, preparing to leave. Jim followed along. Noel stood back, watching.

"You coming back?" Jim asked.

"You want us to?" Ethan replied.

"Yeah. And bring everybody. I've been lonesome for home folk." Jim paused and looked back toward the cabins. "But I love my family, and I love being here. Just bring me some friends."

The conversation ended for a second time. Ethan and Noah rode away on their horses back to where the wagons were camped along the south shore of Long Creek. During the ride back, they were both deep in thought, trying to figure out how they felt about what they had just learned. There was no explanation detailed enough to ease the feeling of betrayal they had felt when Jim Campbell and the colored slave had disappeared.

Finding Jim well was a good thing. But explaining to everyone at camp the situation they had just witnessed was going to be difficult. Ethan was not sure whether he considered Jim a deserter because he had left the survey crew, or whether he still counted him as a friend. Somewhere during the ride he decided he could live in the valley. He would try to convince his family to move farther up the hill above the cabins they had just left.

Noah felt alone. He was never as good a friend to Jim as Ethan was. And he wasn't real cool to the idea of Zeke taking a fake ID, even if it was to gain his freedom. He believed he would go back down to the Big Creek and find a place for his cabin somewhere along the path they had come. He didn't know how to tell Ethan he was leaving Jim Campbell and the Masseys to have the big valley to themselves. He would just go back down stream and pick a spot that looked right to him.

CHAPTER 12

Noah sat on the porch of the cabin, watching the shadows lengthen on the east side of Big Creek. He had just finished putting the last of the wood shingles on the side room. It had been four years since he made the decision to come back down the creek alone.

Arkansas had become a territory in 1819 just about the time they finished the survey and returned to Wayne County, Tennessee.

While Noah and Ethan were surveying, they had no idea people were pouring in from all directions to claim the best land in Arkansas.

Noah remembered how excited Ethan had been about settling at Big Flat, as the area where their base camp had become known. While they debated and planned their return, a trading post was built on the site where they had camped for the last four months they worked on the survey.

Noah watched as the shadows became longer, and he smelled the pan of savory cornbread Emma put in the stove. Four years was a long time, enough time for Noah to settle on the bluff above Big Creek. He had chosen a spot where Hickory Hollow Branch ran into Big Creek. He looked straight across from the porch into another big hollow which had a small stream, and joined Big Creek on the east side.

Emma. Noah thought how much she had changed his life. She had replaced a dream he'd had of bringing his Wayne County sweetheart to Arkansas. The Huckabee family had settled less than half a mile north, on the same side of the creek that Noah had chosen for his cabin. After they filed their claim for the land that joined Noah Sitton, he sat down with Mr. Huckabee to talk about exchanging help to build a cabin. Their 14-year old daughter, who helped by carrying water for them to drink, and had brought lunch every day, became more beautiful each trip she made. Noah began to sit with her away from the crowd while they ate lunch. She was quiet. Noah had always been shy, and tended to wait for Ethan to speak up all the years they had worked together.

The first time Noah and Emma expressed any affection for each other was when he held her hand as she walked across the rocks to cross Hickory Hollow Branch below the cabin they now called their home.

Noah couldn't really remember a proposal of marriage to Emma. He just remembered that one day when they finished working on the Huckabee cabin, Emma said, "When we...." She stopped short before she finished the sentence, blushing as she looked at Noah.

"When you what?" Emma's mother asked.

"When we get married," Noah said. To this day he didn't know how he thought of his answer.

Emma stood and ran to Noah, giving him a hug and looking around at her parents.

Two weeks later, a circuit preacher they had never seen before, and were not even sure he was a preacher, had pronounced them man and wife.

Noah wrote a letter back to Wayne County explaining all about the land that he had acquired. He had been able to get 180 acres. He had four 40-acre tracts set in a square with the center being directly where Hickory Hollow joined Big Creek. He had 20 acres, half of a 40-acre tract, that he had split with the Huckabees to allow them access to the road to Big Flat.

He'd spent quite a bit of time writing the letter describing the land and how he had used the money he'd found in the bottom of the toolbox. "Make sure you take care of that toolbox, and make sure you check the bottom after you get where you're going," his dad told him. He'd not really thought anything about it until one day he tried to find a chisel to cut a notch in a door to attach a hinge, and noticed something shining through the corner of the box. When he removed the bottom, he was shocked to find it was covered with gold coins.

He explained in the letter that he still had quite a lot of the money left, and he had been able to work continuously building the barns and a cabin because he didn't have to trap furs to support himself. After he explained all the progress he had made, he said that he found a place they could come to and have a permanent home.

Noah ended the letter with, "And I married Emma Huckabee. They are the family just north of us, and she is their oldest daughter."

He could have written a description of Emma. He could've written that she was probably 5'4" tall, had beautiful black hair, was a really good cook, and could make and mend clothes. He could also have added that "we will have our first child sometime next March, and if you hurry and come from Tennessee, you can be here by then."

He didn't write any of that.

Ethan had not seen Noah in over a year. After Noah decided to go back down the creek and settle somewhere else besides in the valley now known as Campbell, named after Jim Campbell and the rest of the Campbell family who had settled there. Those first three years they stayed in touch mostly through a fur trader.

Noah had settled into a routine of developing each patch of land along the bluff near the house into a purpose that would provide a particular food. The soft sandy soil in front of the house had become a potato patch. The land behind the house next to the spring that flowed to the south toward Hickory Hollow had become the vegetable patch for beans, squash, and all sorts of vegetables. Emma was a wonderful gardener, a good housekeeper, and could cook.

Noah Sitton was skilled as a blacksmith, a carpenter, a logger, and he could make moonshine. He was your typical Sitton from Wayne County, Tennessee.

The Huckabee clan was from just north of Wayne County, and Noah had heard of them. While it was his first time to actually meet them he discovered they shared the same skills as the Sitton clan, plus they had seed saved for planting everything they needed to survive in a garden.

It seemed to Noah you could make two choices. One, if you depended on fur trade to live, it took a constant effort to follow the game trails and to be able to trap the animals. The other choice was to develop the land, grow crops, grow animals that could be sold for meat, and plant corn for making moonshine.

Noah's letter arrived in Wayne County after only three weeks. Nathaniel Sitton read the letter as the rest of the family listened.

"Are we going?" asked one of the young boys sitting at the other end of the porch with his back to Nathaniel.

Nathaniel Sitton folded the letter, placed it inside the bib pocket of his overalls, and spat into the yard. He slowly turned to his wife and the rest of the Sitton clan.

"Yes, we are going." Nathaniel's answer rang against the walls of the porch and echoed out into the valley in front of them.

It had been almost two years since Noah had written the letter and Nathaniel had read it aloud to all of the Sitton family. They had left in the spring of 1830 and returned after they got to the Mississippi and it was too crowded, too many people waiting to ferry across, and it looked like the river stretched forever.

There was not near the uproar of their return as there had been some years earlier when people had given away everything they had, and then had come back and reclaimed it because they had been afraid to cross the Mississippi.

When they returned this time they still owned some property. They had left it vacant as insurance against not being able to cross the river. The trip to Arkansas had become famous. There were those people who tried and failed, and would never go that direction again. There were those people whose families had split in half, with some moving on to Arkansas, and others choosing to go farther north into Missouri and Kansas.

The Sitton family would settle along Big Creek where Noah had built his cabin. John Rhodes had listened as they talked and planned their trip. He still mourned the loss of Andy, who had fallen off the bluff while surveying. John had thought of going to Arkansas, but his only hope was to find the grave where his son was buried. He knew that Ethan Massey and Noah Sitton could take him to that site.

He walked slowly as she covered the distance toward towards the Sitton place. He could see they had wagons and were getting ready to leave Wayne County. He moved into the shadows of the wagons and came to the front where Nathaniel were repairing the harness for the mules.

"Nate, can we join you?" John asked.

Nathaniel laid the harness down alongside the other sets. He aligned the hames, the two curved pieces of iron or wood which attaches to the collar of all the harnesses in a neat pile, ready to hang on the side of the wagon.

"Yes, you can," answered his old friend of many years. They never had a problem, and Nathaniel didn't believe that John Rhodes blamed either Noah or Ethan for Andy's death.

It would be good to have John Rhodes come along on the journey. Nathaniel Sitton didn't know much about the Rhodes family, except that they always had enough resources to pay their own way. He knew that if they made it to Arkansas, they would have a grist mill for grinding grain, or they would have a sawmill for cutting lumber. They were industrious, hard-working people. Nathaniel Sitton would be glad to travel with these people.

CHAPTER 13

Nathaniel Sitton led the wagons as they left Wayne County and started to Memphis. John Rhodes brought up the rear wagon. There were only nine wagons in this caravan as they traveled toward the Mississippi.

Crossing the Mississippi had not been difficult at all. They were able to catch the ferry the same day they arrived at the landing. Travel had become so common with all the people trying to get to Arkansas the trails were marked and easy to follow.

The only problem was the campsites. They were littered with other travelers leaving behind broken wagon wheels, harnesses in need of repair, and even miscellaneous farm tools. Nathan and John Rhodes looked at all the debris before they decided to go on and make their campsite further down the trail.

Nathaniel wondered how many people had started this trip totally unprepared. He remembered seeing a man leading four pack mules, with his wife and three children walking barefoot along behind the mules.

"Where you headed, my friend?" Nathaniel had walked to the edge of his property where a public road existed. He never intended for it to become a thoroughfare. He had stood looking at the family in clothes that were ragged. The man's shoes had been repaired several times. His wife was barefoot, as were the children. The man didn't answer for quite some time, and then he said one word: "Arkansas."

It had bothered Nathaniel to watch these people leaving on a hopeless march toward a place they had no idea what they would do when they got there.

As they waited to board the ferry, Nathaniel paid for the Sitton wagons, while John Rhodes paid for his family's. Nathaniel's mind flashed back to those people on foot leading pack mules, and he wondered if they had been able to cross the river. He wondered where those people were now.

They traveled across the sandy hills east of Crowley's Ridge and journeyed north to a crossing of the Black River. They planned to stay in Arkansas, traveling along the northern side of the White River until they reached a place known as Nelly's Apron on the White River. Noah had told them there would be a ferry immediately above that which would carry them across the White River and for some distance up the Buffalo River where they would be able to hit the trail, which would be easy for them to come all the way to the Big Creek crossing they needed to take to make it to where they were going.

It had only been 17 days when they made it from the Mississippi to the northern side of White River, close to a new settlement which later became Batesville, Arkansas. Travel was much easier than they expected in 1831 compared to the stories they had heard before 1825. It seemed they passed a continuous building of houses and homesteads being developed almost on every piece of property.

John Rhodes caught up with Nathaniel and said, "Can you believe the survey wasn't finished until 1819. Arkansas became a territory that same year, they elected a territorial governor, and began establishing counties."

Nathaniel stopped and stood still for a moment. "The boys," he referred to Ethan Massey and Noah Sitton, "thought it would take 15 years to get enough people to even have any kind of system or any existence of civilization."

John looked toward the west at the trail as it rounded a curve in the White River. "We better hurry. If I read Ethan's letter right when he wrote to us, and if what Noah has written about how fast the settlers are arriving, we'll be lucky if we find a decent homestead."

"Nathaniel, if I understand the maps and the descriptions accurately, there is a hollow with water, timber, bluffs, and little bottoms of land waiting to be cleared and will make us a decent homestead," John answered.

Nathaniel stood thinking about what John had just said. John had more information, and better and bigger descriptions than he had ever gotten from Noah. Of course, Nathaniel knew how quiet Noah was, and how he never wanted to add details or embellish on any story he ever told. Nathaniel and Noah's mother were always amazed when they read the few letters they had gotten, how little detail he gave them, like when he wrote and said he married Emma Huckabee, he just added, "You need to get here, we're having a baby."

When he thought of Noah's letters, he could believe John would have a better description from the letters Ethan Massey had written, and probably were accurate. But then, he stopped and thought, Noah was the one thoughtful enough to copy all of the survey notes to where they could identify the homesteads they wanted.

But, he remembered reading when Noah had decided to turn and go back down Big Creek, looking for their homestead. He only hoped Noah made a good choice. As they traveled closer every day, the terrain constantly changed, and by the time they made it to the crossing of White River that would take them up the Buffalo, there were huge, rough mountains with smaller mountains filling in the gaps, and small ravines between each of the little ridges.

They ferried across the White River, and landed considerable distance up the Buffalo River. When the wagons all got all lined up and ready to begin their journey on the last leg of the trip to Arkansas, they were in a field which had been cleared and planted in corn.

John and Nathaniel looked at how neat and straight the rows were, and how even the stand of corn was planted. The plants looked healthy, and were growing at a good pace. They felt encouraged. They remembered when they started farming in Wayne County, it looked like that the first couple of years. Then they tried a crop of cotton, not realizing how much nutrients it would take out of the soil. They also did not realize how many hazards there were in growing cotton. Bole weevils had destroyed their second crop. Neither one of the two men had ever owned a slave. They found out the work involved to continually weed and grow cotton was more than typical white farmers could do.

"John, I'm not interested in trying to get enough land to grow anything more than vegetables and corn, and to raise enough livestock for our own use." Nathaniel believed he was ready to do things that would make life simple and easy. He looked forward to homesteading a place where there was a bluff. He had worked with his dad and brothers for years clearing some land that had some rough hillsides above it that they considered unsuitable to clear or try to farm.

He would never forget the winter the Cass family moved in and cleared all of the immediate hillsides above their fields. He would never forget the three weeks of rain that came after Nathaniel and his brothers had finished planting their fields. The cleared hillsides above their fields, that belonged to the Cass family, had eroded every inch of the fields that had just been freshly planted. It was the worst year for every farm in Wayne County. The boys had left to go survey. John Rhodes, Nathaniel Sitton, Earl Massey, and all the other parents had encouraged the boys to go to Arkansas, find some good land, and they could leave these burned out, farmed out, desolate hillsides, and let somebody else figure out what to do with Wayne County, Tennessee.

The decision had been made. They thought the reasons were good. The battle for the last 13 years to get a survey, to go back and forth across the Mississippi to Arkansas, all these things were coming to an end.

Good, bad, or different, the wagons carrying the settlers from Tennessee were making good progress as they traveled along the north bank of the Buffalo River, with a watchful eye to the place where Big Creek flowed in from the south, and the trail that would take them to where the new homes would be.

CHAPTER 14

The crossing of the Buffalo River just above the mouth of Big Creek had been easy. The trail followed the edge of the field of corn, turned and crossed the creek just past a partially finished barn.

Nathaniel liked the looks of the land and of the creek flowing crystal clear with a gravel bottom. The deeper areas of the creek stood in pools deep enough for the fish to hide under the large boulders or underneath the willow covered bank. The trail traveled in the creek bed, at times alternating between being on the gravel and actually in the shallow edge of the water.

He wondered how many years it had taken for the flow of the creek to cut its way to the bottom of the bluffs and create the deep soil for the fields.

These fields appeared to have been cleared for several years, and the brush had been burned. There was no sign of stump holes or any stumps. He wondered if the trees had been oak, or if they had been sycamore, or mostly willows.

The description of the trail Noah had given was very accurate.

Nathaniel stopped the wagons and waited for everyone to gather around before he started his conversation.

"John and I think we're within two or three days travel before we get to the place Noah has settled. I believe, if I'm reading his letter right, we should probably camp where a creek comes in from the east." Nathaniel waited for John Rhodes to reply.

"Nate." John had become accustomed to shortening Nathaniel's name during the trip, and Nathaniel had not objected. "I believe, from what you told me, you're right."

"John, have you noticed how high in the trees some of this driftwood is along the creek?" Nathaniel asked. John looked toward the bluff to the north side of the creek from where they stood. He saw a rather large piece of driftwood lodged 15 or 20 feet above the creek level below.

"You're right, Nate. That's the reason all of the homesteads have been on top of the ledges in the areas where the bluffs are not as tall," John commented.

"I wonder if the buildings Noah has built are sitting on a ledge like that one?" Nathaniel pointed to the top of a roof they could see sitting back some distance away from the edge of the short bluff above them.

John made a sweeping gesture with his right arm, then stopped and pointed at the different ledges they could see which created flat plateaus above the creek bed, but below the mountains sitting behind them.

"I have never seen anything like it," John said as he lowered his arm after having pointed at the bluffs. "We could have bottomland along the creek and we could have bench land next to the house, which would never flood, and we could keep our animals away from the creek.

"That's the way I think Noah described where he built the house." Nathaniel referred to the place where he expected to arrive sometime later in the week.

The trip had seemed short for the last three days as they continued their travel up Big Creek looking for the place Noah had described. It was almost dark when they arrived below the bluff, and Nathaniel had yelled for Noah at the top of his lungs. His voice echoed off the bluffs and hollows, and the sound of Noah answering was mixed in with the echoes as they faded away.

Everyone deserted their wagons and scrambled up the foot trail to the top of the ledge where Noah's voice had come from.

Noah walked toward them. Emma followed, carrying a child on her hip. Noah's mother stared. She could not believe how mature her boy appeared to be as he walked toward her.

He was a husky man, his sandy hair had taken on a deeper brown color. His face, which had stayed smooth, now showed a scraggly beard trying to cover it. His clothes were clean, and he carried himself like a man, with pride and confidence. And then he broke into a run, grabbed his mother and gave her a hug.

Dark settled in before they had said all their greetings and met their new granddaughter and daughter-in-law, and began taking a tour of all the neat building Noah had constructed for the Sitton homestead.

John Rhodes was quiet, his family stood back and watched as the Sittons got reacquainted, not only with each other, but with their new surroundings. It would be a few days before the Rhodes family could make a decision on where their new home would be.

The Rhoades chose a place to homestead. They would build a gristmill just like they had in Tennessee. Nathaniel Sitton could not believe that he had agreed to help build a mill pond. He was in charge of chinking and sealing the rocks while the younger guys carried them and put them in place. It took almost a week to excavate the area where John Rhodes wanted to capture the water from a spring flowing out from under the bluff.

They finally got an area, probably 60 feet wide at its widest point, just before the water ran over the edge of a lower section of bluff. They left a stream flowing across the middle and running over the edge of the bluff that would eventually be dammed up with large boulders to create the mill pond.

John Rhodes knew what he was doing. He had left one of these mill ponds in the mountains of Wayne County, in an almost identical setting.

"Nate, this will be a lot better than the one I had." John smiled with pride as he looked at the area they were building. This pool would hold the water which would be released and turn the waterwheel for his new gristmill. He brought the gears and shaft with him. The wheel would have to be built from lumber here in Arkansas. The grinding stones for the gristmill were coming in another wagon train bringing additional equipment and supplies, along with more families who would settle here.

The work was hard, but neighbors had joined the efforts. When Ethan Massey heard they were in the area, he made a trip to see who had arrived from Wayne County. Another reunion of old friends took place along the banks of another creek named Cedar Creek, the place where the grist mill was being built.

All the clans shared the work for most of the summer. In 1831 in Arkansas, along the creeks which fed into Big Creek and made their way to the Buffalo River, were becoming very populated. The Masseys, the Martins, the Campbells, the Morrisons, along with the Sittons, all settled in, their homesteads close together.

There were conflicts over whose property was whose, and a lot of the paperwork and descriptions of the land was totally inaccurate. The Campbells had homesteaded and built their houses, and had deeds. When Ethan and Noah checked their fieldnotes and descriptions, they had settled on land that the Morrison family had paperwork for.

When they began to try to straighten out the paperwork, the trip to the land office, and signing new documents which gave the property to the people who actually lived on it, was all it took to clear it up.

"We better be proud this wasn't some of the folks we lived next to back in Tennessee and other parts of the country," John Rhodes commented after it was all settled and his gristmill was grinding grain for the cornbread they would eat all winter.

It had been a long journey covering several years, but 1831 was the new beginning for the settlers from Wayne County, Tennessee. They were now settled in Arkansas.

CHAPTER 15

It seemed like only yesterday when Nathaniel Sitton and John Rhodes made their final stop along Cedar Creek, and four miles farther down on Big Creek where Noah had built the original Sitton homestead.

It was a frosty October morning in 1843, the year that the counties were divided and formed, seven years after Arkansas became a state. It was almost breathtaking, how fast the hills had been settled and become homesteads. The Sitton family had always been moonshiners, and when they moved to Arkansas, it was only natural they searched for the perfect place to set up a still.

Noah hunted along the bluffs on both sides of Big Creek. He stood on the ledge just below where Bratton Creek joined Big Creek. He looked around and wondered what was above him, when he spotted a crack in the larger bluff. He explored, and discovered that if you went to the crack, it was actually a crevice about ten feet wide, which traveled at an angle until you were on top of the section.

When he walked out on top, he realized it was just another level, and there was also a bluff some 20 feet tall encircling the area after you went through the crevice.

He walked around and discovered there was a cave going 20 feet or farther into the hill. Inside the cave was a spring which surfaced and ran very few feet before disappearing into a crevice. Noah had never worked at making moonshine, but when he looked around, his first thoughts were if his dad wanted to make whiskey after he got there, this would be the place to do it.

It would be possible to bring a small wagon through the crevice to the top of the ledge. And the bluff would conceal all the barrels and supplies for making moonshine. As he looked at the bluff to the right of the cave, he could see it was possible to build a boiler next to the bluff, and the smoke would be diffused over a wide area before it rose up into the trees. He remembered when moonshiners tried to steal or destroy other people's stills, they located them by tracking the smoke as it rose in a little straight spiral, giving away the exact location. That would not happen here.

It had been ten years since Noah had shown the site to Nathaniel. When Asa Sitton arrived in 1834, one of the first things Nathaniel did was take him to the place Noah had shown him for a still. Noah had helped locate the tract of land on the map of the area.

When they went to the land office, the clerk asked, "Why would you want that land? It's just cedars and rocks."

Nathaniel and Asa did not comment. They just paid the $16 for 40 acres, and filed for the deed.

Noah had never worked building or developing the still. His mother totally disagreed with what his father did when he made moonshine. She never objected to spending any of the money he made from selling the moonshine, though.

"How do we separate our moral convictions when we participate in the profits?" Noah wondered.

He was always busy. He and Emma now had five children, three boys and two girls. Emma worked with all the other families trying to start a school on the east side of Big Creek, on top of a ledge with a smaller tract of land than where Noah built their house. Noah and most of the other men from the surrounding area, of about a three-mile radius, erected a one-room structure which became the schoolhouse.

They taught school from the fourth of July weekend until the middle of August, the period of time when the crops were laid by. That time period was when crops were no longer plowed, and there was no need to pull weeds. But by the end of August, it was time to harvest all the corn, and gather seeds for the next planting.

All of the settlers had adjusted to their own routines. John Rhodes' family had grown by adding in-laws as fast as the children became of marrying age. That could mean a 14-year-old girl and a 16-year-old boy, quite common among the settlers of north Arkansas.

Noah thought back to the time when he and Ethan Massey marched with Colonel Jackson to New Orleans. He was born in 1800 and had fought in the Battle of New Orleans in 1814. Ethan was only a couple of years older, and Jim Campbell was probably another three years older. When they joined the survey, Noah was the youngest member of the crew in 1816. He was not sure how old Andy Rhodes had been when he fell off the bluff and died during the survey.

He walked away from the creek and sat down on the edge of the porch. He continued to reminisce about what had happened since the first time he came to Arkansas. He thought of all the disappointments. He thought of all the successful things that had happened. He stood up and walked toward the northeast corner of the property, and peered over the bluff into Hickory Hollow. He remembered the day he decided the hog pen needed to be located below the little bluff some eight or nine feet tall. He had checked the shelter which would be available for the hogs to stay in cold weather, and in the summer if they wanted to get out of the heat. And he extended the fence to where it took in a small corner of the stream, hardly more than a trickle, but big enough to provide water for the hogs.

It was easy to feed there because he could dump the corn, or whatever he was feeding them, without actually going into the pen. There was no chance of the noise or odor ever being heard or smelled at the house.

Noah walked the entire circle around what had been his and Emma's home until his family had joined him. Straight across the creek in a hollow they named George's Holler was where Nathaniel and his mother built their cabin. As Noah continued to look at each hollow, he could see the rooftops of other family members' houses who had settled at the Sitton homestead.

Noah thought about the paperwork. He had the original deed for 180 acres, and it was Noah Sitton and heirs. As he looked at the houses, he realized there was no possibility of determining who owned what. His two younger brothers had built their houses where the springs came out above their house. The water flowed past their houses, and was used for the animal lots as it flowed through. It was the same at his house, his dad's house, and all the other people along the creek.

In 1843 houses were placed wherever the water flowed out of a crevice and could be developed as a spring providing water for household needs. Noah stood thinking. "We've got people homesteading the tops of these ridges, and carrying water over a quarter of a mile to supply their needs. It won't work."

Things had changed quickly. The bountiful game and furs were no longer in existence. The occasional elk which was seen during the survey years, and harvested by the Cherokees when they settled along the southern banks of

White River, were no more. Noah heard rumors from the Indians and the early trappers while they had been doing the survey, that buffalo were actually in the area, and the Buffalo River was named for a herd.

1843. Noah reminisced about the first 43 years of his life. He wondered what would happen over the next 20 years. He was young enough, and had seen enough things happen to know there would be big changes, even here in Arkansas.

While Noah was having these thoughts Ethan was at his home in the Campbell community over 6 miles south of Noah's and was sitting on the porch of his cabin facing west. He could see the results of his 20 years' work. He watched as his two sons, a 16-year-old and a 14-year-old, plowed the fields for the first time without him being with them.

It had been a good time for the Masseys who had settled in the place now known as Campbell. It was named for Jim Campbell, and that was appropriate, given that he was the one who had developed most of the area. Several families from Wayne County had settled in the valley which was a huge hollow at the head of a creek now named Sellers.

Jim Campbell had shown a lot of consideration when people arrived, by making sure their new homestead was in an appropriate place, and would not conflict with their neighbors. The Morrison family had settled at the upper end of the valley next to the bluff. The land on top of the hill was now known as Oxley. Ethan was not sure how many families had settled on Oxley Mountain.

Although he was several miles away, Ethan's thoughts turned to Noah Sitton. He had seen Noah several times at the John Rhodes' gristmill on Cedar Creek. It was always good to see his old friend.

"I've got to see Noah." He thought about the stranger who had shown up, questioning him about Zeke, the colored slave who had joined Jim when he left the survey crew.

"I am here to recover my client's property. Runaway slaves," the man had stated.

Ethan didn't know what procedure the man planned on taking to try to re-enslave Zeek. He wondered how a man who had lived free for over 20 years, and raised a family who was now very much a part of a community would react if someone decided he had to return to a plantation in Mississippi. "I've got to discuss this with Noah."

Ethan left early, before daylight, rode down Sellers Creek, and crossed to the north side of the long creek arm of Big Creek. He rode a bay horse which he had bought in Wiley's Cove from the Watts family. The horse was definitely a good mount. He could ride the horse to the edge of the creek bank, and it would stand there perfectly still while he watched the fish swimming in the deep, clear waters of one of the pools. He would mark the place and decide if he was going to come back and harvest a mess of fish.

The settlers had adopted the Indians' method of fishing by spearing the fish with a three- prong metal gig at the end of a pole. It was not necessary to wait for the fish to bite when you could spear them from the creek bank, and after several pitches of the gig, you had enough for a really good fish fry.

He rode on, realizing he was wasting time when he needed to hurry on down the creek to see Noah.

After the visit with Ethan, Noah leaned back in his chair and stared at the bluff across the creek. He watched a hawk circling an area directly between his house and his dad's. He thought about what Ethan had just told him. He had always been bothered by the deceit of Zeke taking another man's identity, even if the paper would gain him his freedom.

Ethan hadn't left out any of the details about Jim Campbell's and Zeke's families.

"They're good people, Noah," had been Ethan's description after he told about the oldest girl and boy from Zeke's marriage with the Indian girl. They were married into the Hayes family and had children .

"Don't it matter to those folks that those kids are half Indian and part colored?" Noah asked.

Ethan looked down at the blue tick pup lying in front of the porch where he and Noah sat. He could see a touch of Chase's black and tan blood in the pups. He was still proud that Chase had made it all the way from Wayne County, and after 20 years was the sire of more good dogs throughout Arkansas than any dog to ever arrive. He felt silly for a moment. How could he be looking at the dog when he hadn't answered the question?

He thought about how that pup had no control over the sire or the grandsire that he came from. Ethan stood and stretched his arms out away from his body. "We don't see color in the Campbell community." After a pause he added, "We see people with the purpose in our lives."

Noah stood up and joined him, the dog trailing behind, as they walked toward the bluff on the west side of Big Creek. They stood on the ledge with its sandy little bottom of land between the edge and the cabin. Noah thought about how little he actually knew about Zeke. Although he lived less than ten miles from the Campbell community, he knew problems would spread like wildfire. There had never been a report of a problem in that community.

"What are we going to do if we are asked to testify in some kind of hearing?" Noah asked.

"I don't know," answered Ethan.

The visit ended with Ethan riding away at a slower pace than when he came. Noah walked slowly back to the house, deep in thought. "We can't tell a lie in court if it comes to that," he said just above a whisper.

Ethan continued to think about their conversation, problems have a way of hiding until it's time to cause the most trouble, Ethan thought as he rode his horse across the creek, for the first of many crossings before he would be back in the Campbell community.

He observed what had been accomplished since they arrived in the valley over 20 years ago. Along the creek there were fields where they should never have been cleared. There were cabins that washed away in floods. But, overall, it had become prosperous farmland with neighbors learning to live after the bounty of furs and timber were harvested.

He still loved the sounds as dark started to come at the end of the day. The whippoorwills were always somewhere in the distance. The sight of otter and mink coming out to feed on fish in the stream always seemed to slither away just as he saw them. He looked up at the bright sky still in the light at the treetops. If he hurried, he could be home before dark.

He sat down on his porch and visited with Sarah, but he could not give her any details about going to see Noah. It was their burden to share between them, two friends who had endured many things together. A trip to New Orleans with Colonel Jackson. Three years spent surveying swamps, hills, bluffs, and valleys. All part of their trip to Arkansas. He thought of all the times when maybe they should have given up. But now they had a different problem; how to support a legal system of property and protect a friend in the community at the same time.

Noah's thoughts were almost identical, some ten miles away, as he tossed corn over the edge of the bluff into the hog pen. It always seemed he could find answers while he was doing a chore. This time was different. He could not answer a problem that he didn't know anything about. He knew that he and Ethan would not tell a lie, but at the same time they were not going to volunteer anything beyond the questions they may be asked.

CHAPTER 16

Jim Campbell read the paper three times. It had been issued by the circuit court judge for the county of Searcy and the state of Arkansas. The claim had been filed on behalf of a plantation headquartered in Mississippi with holdings in the southeast corner of Arkansas.

The paper alleged that a slave by the name of Zeke had not returned after completing his work for the survey company. It went on to describe how Zeke had represented himself to be a free man, and was living in Searcy County under false pretenses.

" Jim, what is there that can be done?" Zeke asked after the sheriff delivered the paper.

After reading it, Jim determined it was a court order to appear at the courthouse in Marshall on the 15th of the month of October. Zeke left the paper with Jim.

Jim saddled his horse, and with the paper in his pocket, he began the ride to Ethan's house. Ethan Massey always seemed to have the best plans. It had been over two and a half years since the detective, or whomever the man was, had come around saying he was there to recover his boss's property.

Ethan read the paper. "It's what I've been expecting, but why did it take this long for them to file their claim?"

Zeke had followed Jim, and was now standing in the yard looking up at Ethan and Jim.

Ethan looked down into the face of his friend. He had never thought of him as anyone's property, and he couldn't understand how after over thirty years someone would come and try to take him back to the plantation.

Ethan's first thought was to go back and see Noah. After some discussion with Jim and Zeke, it was agreed that Ethan would go and talk to the county prosecutor, and, if he could, to the judge who issued the order.

"Ethan, let's hire a lawyer." Jim turned and put his hand on Zeke's shoulder. "I don't know what we can do, but we're going to try to keep you here where you are."

Zeke didn't say anything. He just walked away. His steps were slow. He wondered why he couldn't just present the papers he had that said he was a free slave by the name of Noel Milam. When they found those papers many years ago, Jim Campbell had handed them to him with excitement saying, "Zeke, you're a free man. You are now Noel Milam."

After Ethan and Noah met, they had a conversation at the gristmill. They talked about the papers Noel Milam had been carrying when they found him dead, and decided they couldn't claim the identity of those papers.

"Dad says if you ever try to present those false papers in court as legal documents "added Noah, "you will be in more trouble than you will be trying to get Zeke's freedom some other way."

Ethan rode in the best buggy the Massey clan owned. Sarah sat beside him, anxious to shop when they got to Marshall. 1850 had seen a couple of stores open during the construction of the new courthouse, after the county seat was moved from Lebanon to Marshall. The courthouse was almost completed, and the judge's office was on the first floor. Ethan was curious to find out if his questions could be answered.

Was there a time limit for claiming Zeke as property? Did it matter that he was married and had raised a family, and those children were now married with children? These questions and more went through his mind as Sarah sat talking constantly about what she would like to buy while she was in town.

For the most part, Ethan and Jim Campbell had not discussed Zeke's problem with any of the other people in the Campbell community. Ethan smiled. "I had absolutely forgotten that Zeke was a slave, that he was colored, and that his wife left her Indian tribe to live and raise a family with a slave."

Ethan knew absolutely nothing about slavery. The Masseys had never owned a slave. Their part of Tennessee was not cotton country, and the only people who ever owned a slave were the Bryants who moved there from Alabama. They had a young man, and a younger woman. The young man worked with Mr. Bryant at whatever job he was doing at the time.

Ethan remembered how skilled he seemed to be, whether they were in the blacksmith shop sharpening tools, or whether they were mending harnesses, or working on wagons and other equipment. He had never thought of them in terms of slavery, either. They had lived in quarters attached to the main house after the Bryants finished remodeling. The Bryant children were raised by these colored servants. It was Ethan's only knowledge or experience until he joined the survey crew and they were given slaves contracted to work as helpers.

His mind flashed back to the day he said goodbye to his colored friend who had worked with him the entire time during the survey. The slave had learned to read and write. Ethan thought he was Zeke's brother, but he could not remember the name he called his colored friend.

Ethan then remembered how upset they became when Andy Rhodes fell off the bluff while trying to plumb bob the survey line over the bluff. He was holding on to the measuring chain when he slipped and fell. The crew had scrambled, trying to get around and down to where Andy landed.

Ethan arrived in Marshall and tied the horse to the hitching rail, alongside the other buggies parked below the courthouse. He went inside and laid the paper on the judge's desk after he was asked by the judge to come in and tell him what he needed.

Ethan stood quietly. The judge picked up the paper and read it.

"I didn't have a choice," the judge began. "The lawyer for the plantation owner presented affidavits from the survey company that Zeke was hired to them for the duration of the survey and was to be returned to their possession at the end of the survey." The judge stood and walked to the window that had been installed in the wall a few weeks earlier. He looked out at the street.

"That plantation has an unbelievable amount of land in Mississippi, and they have bought most of Chico County in southeast Arkansas. They are trying to buy and recover all the slave labor they can get." The judge turned back from the window and faced Ethan. "The old man who started the plantation many years ago passed it on to two sons with the understanding they would not abuse or mistreat the slaves. A great grandson now owns the plantation," the judge commented. "I've written letters for over two years trying to prevent having to issue that order." He pointed to the piece of paper still lying on the desk.

"What can we do?" Ethan asked. He used the term "we" as an all-inclusive word for all the people in the Campbell community who knew that losing Zeke and however many other family members would be a major loss.

"Ethan, you hire Joel Bratton as Zeke's attorney." The judge sat down. "I don't know if I can conduct this hearing. I am prejudiced, and have made up my mind. But if we have a hearing, I believe the law will be on the plantation owner's side."

Ethan sat down. He picked up the piece of paper and placed it in his pocket. "Where is Joel Bratton's office?" He fumbled with a note pad lying on the desk.

"Hand me that notepad," said the judge as he reached toward Ethan. The judge placed it on the desk and began to write. He folded the note when he finished writing and handed it to Ethan. "Don't you read that, Ethan. You just go across the street and give it to Joel." He stood and pointed out the window toward the building directly across the street from the judge's office.

After leaving Joel Bratton's office, Ethan searched for Sarah. "How can you lose your wife when there's only two stores for her to be shopping in?" Ethan was not known for patience.

It had been over six months since Ethan had gone to Marshall, seen the judge, and given the note to the attorney.

"Go home, Ethan. Tell Zeke, Jim Campbell, and everybody else to keep their mouth shut until you hear from me," the attorney said when Ethan left his office.

Ethan had given Noah an update about what was going on, and let Noah read the paperwork he had picked up at the Sheriff's office.

There were several pages on record explaining the plantation owner's claim. It had taken a while for the clerk to copy all of those papers and give them to Ethan. The edges were beginning to wear after all the times Jim, Ethan, Noah, and Zeke had tried to make sense of them.

Ethan and Noah met several times. They still didn't have a plan, and they still had not heard from the attorney.

Time would tell. Or would it? That was always the question when you lived in north Arkansas.

CHAPTER 17

Noah sat watching the small crystal-clear pool of water along the Hickory Hollow branch, just above where it ran through the corner of his hog pen. He saw a top water minnow, a small minnow with a spot in the center of its head directly in front of its eyes. They were named top waters because they always swam immediately below the surface of the water.

Noah had stopped to watch because the day before he had noticed a smallmouth bass close to 12 inches long swimming in the pool, going in and out from under the bank. He wondered how long the top water minnow would survive before it became food for the bass. He wondered how the minnow had gotten into the pool, since it did not flow continuously to Big Creek. The stream in Hickory Hollow sank into the gravel almost a mile above the hog pen. Very little water ever flowed in the streambed the rest of the way. Noah and Ethan had discovered a really cold spring which came into a large hole of water a quarter mile upstream from the mouth of Hickory. They also discovered one day the source was Hickory Hollow after a downpour at the head above the big springs in the hollow made the water hole almost muddy.

They had also discovered that a number of the crevices in the bluff led to a cavern with a stream of water flowing through it before it disappeared into Big Creek. Noah was sure there had to be a cave somewhere along the bluffs above where he stood.

Noah walked along the small stream, trying to clear his head after a visit with Ethan. Zeke and Ethan had just left the Sitton homestead. They had brought a copy of an order issued by the judge for the hearing to determine the ownership of a colored slave known in the Campbell community area as Zeek.

Ethan had read aloud the lines of the letter which Joel Bratton, the attorney, had written and sent with the deputy sheriff when he delivered the notice.

Joel had written, "It appears the plaintiff," and it listed the plantation owner, "has furnished enough documentation to justify hearing of ownership." Joel also added, "We will not answer the complaint until all of this is on the record." He had gone on to include a summary of the law protecting slave ownership that had just passed the US Congress. "It will be difficult to keep Zeke here," Joel added.

It had been a hard conversation for Ethan and Noah to have in Zeke's presence.

"Does I have to go back?" Zeke asked continuously while they read the letter and discussed the problem.

Noah did not have any idea how this problem could be solved. After walking several yards upstream, he returned to the pool where the top water minnow had been swimming. The minnow was gone.

"Life is cruel, just like when Andy fell off the bluff, just like when the minnow was swallowed by the bass," Noah said softly.

Noah never claimed understanding how things happened. He wasn't nearly as vested in the outcome of Zeke's hearing as Ethan was. The people living in the Campbell community were all involved in each other's families and lives.

Zeke's children were married to members of at least four different families in the area. His oldest daughter lived on Oxley Mountain, married to a Hayes boy. They had three children. Noah didn't know the circumstances of the other three children, but he was sure the situation was basically the same.

He stepped across the small stream trickling out of the pool before it disappeared again into the gravel. The next time the stream would be noticeable would be the pool it created in the corner of the hog lot. The stream always flowed clear and cool, and looked perfect. Ethan walked around the hog lot, checking the fence to make sure the last flood had not caused any damage. He remembered one spring when a log floated down with the floodwaters and completely destroyed a section of the hog pen. Today he wished the problem with Zeke was no bigger than the job of repairing the hog pen.

Ethan and Noah agreed they would attend the hearing to determine Zeke's ownership.

After they read Joel's statement that he would not prepare an answer to the complaint until after the evidence of ownership was presented, Noah waited for Ethan's opinion.

Zeke walked to his horse and mounted up. He did not hear their comments.

"I don't see any way to fight this," Ethan said.

"I don't, either," Noah answered. He started his walk as Ethan and Zeke rode away. It'd probably been over an hour since he had first stopped at the pool of water and watched the top water minnow swimming in a peaceful circle. The time had not provided any ideas or answers to the problem.

Joel had concluded the letter attached to the orders from the judge by stating, "Bring everyone to the hearing who might strengthen our case."

Noah always tried to avoid controversy. He did not want to become involved with a decision that was going to be a problem. But he was beginning to hear rumblings every time he was around other people of the dispute over slavery. It appeared the tradition of slavery and the profiteering from the colored people's labors, and trading them as if they were animals was about to end.

Over the next several weeks, before Saturday, April 17, 1852, the day for the hearing in Marshall, Arkansas, Noah heard continuous plans being made by people to attend the hearing. He decided he would have to go himself. He finally explained to his father, Nathaniel, the entire situation. He left nothing out, including when Jim Campbell and Zeke found the dead slave. He told Nathaniel how they reported the slave had died from a gunshot wound to the back of his head. He told how they found the papers giving Noel Milam his freedom. He also told him the hesitant feeling he got in his stomach with the idea that Zeke had taken the identity of a dead man.

Nathaniel wasn't critical of Noah, Jim, Ethan, or Zeke. "Son, people always do whatever they feel they have to do to protect themselves."

Noah walked away from that meeting with his dad, realizing that while he had an interest, he also would not lose anything. The problem was six miles to the south and east from the Sitton homestead.

They made plans to go to the hearing, and Nathaniel said, "We'll take my buggy." They expected to be just part of a larger crowd there to witness the spectacle that would not have a happy ending.

CHAPTER 18

Nathaniel Sitton, even though he was an elderly man with a son who was past fifty, had no trouble getting up early and getting the buggy ready to go. He sat waiting for Noah to come out of his house to join him for their trip to Marshall, the county seat of Searcy County.

He thought back to the years in Tennessee and before that, the time his father and grandfather had spent in Virginia and North Carolina. Slaves had always been a part of the plantation system scattered throughout the south. Now the discussion had become: was it morally right?

Nathaniel's thoughts went back to the teachings he'd heard all his life, mostly from the Bible. He had always wondered about the writings about manservants and different descriptions of slavery. Now he was going to a trial in circuit court where the argument was going to be if the slave owner had the right to own and take possession of another human being. Zeke had been living free for over thirty years.

It was a problem to get from Big Creek in northeastern

Searcy County to Marshall, the county seat. They would travel west along Hickory Hollow until the trail became too narrow and rugged for a wagon. They climbed the hill and followed the ridge several miles before turning south into Barren Hollow. Occasionally the hollow would become flooded after a heavy rain, but for the most part it was always dry. They followed the gravel creek bed before the road was turning south and climbing a hill to a point where on a level with Marshall. From there the road was well traveled, and an easy trip.

There had been very little conversation during the trip. Noah sat confused, wondering how this court case could be argued. If he understood the note from Joel Bratton to Zeke, there was not going to be any real argument, Zeke's attorney was just insisting the plantation owner prove his ownership.

They arrived at the courtyard, circled around the building looking for a place to park the buggy. When they could not find a parking place, they went down the hill to the town spring and parked the buggy. It had always been the watering hole for teams and animals after the trip to town.

As they walked up to the courthouse, they passed by an elaborate carriage. "That thing looks like a funeral buggy, or a hearse," was Nathaniel's comment as they walked by.

"Why does he need the little fringes and curtains?" asked Noah.

Nathaniel looked back at the matched team of gray-black horses with deep, dark manes and tails. "What kind of horses are they?" he asked.

"I don't know," answered Noah. He stared at the harnesses which were deep black leather with brass trim, and the bridles decorated with tassels to match those around the buggy. In addition, it appeared that the knobs on the horses' harnesses could be gold. Or just highly polished brass.

"I don't know why you would need anything like that." Nathaniel continued to study the horses and the carriage as they passed.

They watched as two slaves, dressed in identical uniforms with matching narrow brimmed hats, moved to the front of the wagon and held the horses as the crowd increased around them.

Noah turned to his dad and said, "Joel told Ethan to have you and me come in the side door of the basement. He wants to talk to us before we go up for the hearing."

They entered the basement, and immediately went into a small office where Joel Bratton sat with Ethan Massey, his father Earl, Jim Campbell, and Zeke, the subject of today's hearing. He was using the judges office.

After they were seated, Joel Bratton, the attorney, addressed the small group. "The only thing we can do is insist the plantation owner prove his claim." He stood, walked to the little window, the only source of light coming into the dingy, dark basement room, and looked out. "There's a crowd here that wants to see slavery enforced and upheld. There's also a crowd here who wants Zeke to stay free and live his life as he has for the last thirty years.

"Judge Crawford has written numerous letters asking for further proof before he would grant this hearing," Joel explained. "It has gotten to the point there is no choice but to grant the hearing, based on the original purchase of Zeke in the slave auction at New Orleans, and affidavits of ownership for all the other slaves he contracted to the survey, including Zeke's brother who was a member of the survey team."

"Was that slave named Ross?" asked Ethan.

Zeke spoke up. "Yes sir, he's the one you taught to read and write."

Joel sat back down. He folded his hands. "We are going upstairs. I'm going to question and ask for every claim to be proven as much as possible."

They climbed the stairs, entered the hallway, climbed another set of stairs, and finally came to the hearing room on the top floor of the almost finished courtroom. There was some areas lacking trim, and the floors were just rough sawn lumber, still needing sanded and stained.

Joel, Ethan, his dad, Earl, and Zeke went to a table with chairs, on the left side of the courtroom, facing the judge's bench. Nathaniel Sitton and Noah Sitton split up and walked over to the south wall. They stood with their backs to the wall, looking across the courtroom toward where Joel and Zeke, along with Ethan and Earl Massey, were seated.

Noah looked around the room. While there must've been 100 people assembled together for the hearing, other than the families living in the Campbell community who were seated directly behind Zeke and Joel, he hardly recognized anyone.

The court clerk stood and said, "All rise," as Judge Crawford entered from the side room.

Noah was not sure he'd ever seen the Judge before. He certainly didn't recognize this tall, fair headed gentleman who was getting close to becoming bald. He looked ill at ease in the robe he wore. His necktie was poorly tied and was shifted to one side in his shirt collar. He looked like someone who dressed in a hurry, and was not the least bit anxious to conduct a hearing.

After the judge was seated, he read a statement that the purpose of the hearing was to determine the ownership of a slave named Zeek who had lived in the Campbell community of Searcy County for over thirty years, he has raised a family of children, and presently has grandchildren living in the same community, without any problems or ever having it mentioned that he was a slave.

Noah whispered to his dad, "Does that mean anything?"

Nathaniel did not answer.

Noah did not hear the name of the plantation owner, but when the judge read the rest of the filings for the hearing, he stated that, "this man is here to prove that he is the valid owner of Zeke, a runaway slave that has been living at large in Arkansas since the time of the survey, and he has tried to cover up his actual status as a slave owned by Reynolds Plantation of south Mississippi."

Judge Crawford said, "You may introduce yourself and may begin your presentation to support your claim."

For the next thirty minutes the attorney for the plantation, a tall fellow, slender, with a mixture of reddish-brown hair, wearing a dark blue suit and shoes that were of a quality Noah had never seen before, presented the case for his client.

Noah looked at the plantation owner. He appeared to be shorter than Noah, and was dressed in a white silk suit, and a silk shirt with ruffles where the collar should be. He also wore the largest white, wide-brimmed hat Noah had ever seen.

Judge Crawford asked him to remove the hat a least three times during the thirty minutes, and he immediately put it back on, also trying to relight the cigar the judge asked him to stop smoking.

The plantation owner smiled broadly at those people who smiled at him, and occasionally waved. He frowned and made gestures toward people he thought didn't support his claim. This went on the entire time his attorney presented various pieces of paper, asking the judge to read them aloud, and then asking they be made a part of the record.

Finally, Judge Crawford stepped in. "Sir, you have made your point repeatedly, and I believe I understand that your claim is that Zeke is your property, and that you have a right to recover him and return him to the plantation in Mississippi?"

Before the attorney could answer, the plantation owner jumped to his feet, removed the big hat, and almost screamed, "That slave is mine! I bought him, or, my grand daddy did, and I am taking him back to the plantation, and he's gonna work double until he has done enough work to pay me back for the trouble he has caused!"

Several people shouted their support for the plantation owner. An equal number yelled that no man should ever own another man.

The battle of slavery had made it to a courtroom in Marshall, Arkansas.

Judge Crawford banged his gavel and yelled for order repeatedly. The crowd finally quieted.

"Sir, do you have a value in dollars that you place upon this property?" Judge Crawford asked.

The attorney for the Reynolds Plantation whispered to his client. But before he could answer the judge, the plantation owner yelled, "He's worth $1,700 to me, or he's not worth a cent!"

Judge Crawford leaned forward, looking through all the paperwork laying on the bench.

The plantation owner and his attorney whispered back and forth.

A gentleman from the Leslie community, some few miles south of Marshall, stepped forward and addressed the plantation owner. "Am I understanding that for $1,700 you will release Zeke from his servitude?"

The whispering between the plantation owner and his attorney became intense.

"Not a cent less," was the answer.

Ned Hayes was a man known throughout the county. He operated one of the better farms, a flour mill, and several other businesses. Loud enough for everybody to hear he said, "Your Honor, hold this hearing. I'll be right back."

Judge Crawford stood and said, "We are in recess."

"Do you think he's gone to get the money?" Noah wondered where Mr. Hayes could go for money on a Saturday afternoon. The bank closed at 11 a.m. every Saturday. It was almost 3 p.m.

Before Nathaniel could answer, they heard steps on the stairs.

Mr. Hayes returned, holding several bills in his right hand. He asked the gentleman from Mississippi to come forward to the judge's bench. Joel and Zeke followed a few steps behind.

Mr. Hayes began to count, saying each number loudly. When he reached $1,700, he did not stop. He counted out $300 more for a total of $2,000. He turned and addressed the plantation owner.

"We are going to prepare a bill of sale for your property of Zeke, one slave, and we are paying you the $1,700 you asked for, and I am adding $300 for your expense and trouble to come to Searcy County, and you will sign an affidavit to never set foot in this part of Arkansas again."

When he finished that statement, he turned to Joel and Zeke. "Prepare a release for Zeke from any servitude or any contract of ownership that any person may have, and I will sign it."

Zeke hugged Joel Bratton, his attorney, and then in tears he went to his family, who had been sitting quietly all day during the hearing.

Noah and Nathaniel started their ride home, aware that they would probably be traveling in the dark before they got there.

"Son, this is not the end of this," said Nathaniel. "Zeke got his freedom, but the fight for who is going to win is just starting. Freedom of the slaves may destroy our country."

Noah didn't answer. He didn't like any of it. He didn't like slavery. He didn't like the arrogance of people trying to dominate other people, and telling them what they get or what they couldn't own. He sat in deep thought. He thought about the dreams of moving from Tennessee to get away from the problems. He had just spent the day watching the problems which had followed them to Arkansas.

CHAPTER 19

The summer after the trial seemed to drag on forever. Noah spent the summer working the cornfields along the banks of the creeks. It was a good season, the crops were lush and green, and it appeared the harvest was going to be a good one.

1852 had set the tone early with the argument over the ownership of a man who had lived free for over 30 years. Ethan stayed close to home in the Campbell community, and so had everyone else following all the confusion after the trial.

Noah stood looking at the spring flowing out from under the crevice some 75 yards behind the Sitton houses. The original cabin he had built before Nathan and the rest arrived was dwarfed by the other house. Noah had three brothers and a sister who arrived with his parents.

When he walked to the bluff below the spring and looked across Big Creek, above the mouth of Hickory Hollow, he could see the roofs of their houses. It had been a busy twenty years.

He paused and looked at the narrow, swift stream of water below the spring box. It began to spread out as it descended over the ledges below the spring. The water eventually formed a curtain some 60 feet wide at the point where it went off the bluff. Nathan did not like that and it was a hazard for livestock that ventured out on the slick rock to try drinking water too shallow to drink, and which would freeze in winter, creating an even slicker hazard.

While studying the water flowing away from the spring, he thought about the attempts he had made to redirect the flow. He had created a rock and earthen wall to channel the water into an area south of where the water went over the edge of the bluff. A huge spring rain brought water down both sides of the spring box, washing away everything he had done.

He walked slowly back up the hill toward the spring to a place where the bluff outcropping began to create the narrow channel 75 feet below the spring. As he looked, it occurred to him that if he could cut through the bluff enough to re-channel the flow, he wouldn't have to worry about a flood wiping out his work. He thought about how much work it would be to drill holes into the limestone and blast a channel similar to the millrace at John Rhodes' gristmill. It was something to think about.

The time he'd spent walking and looking at the spring and observing the changes since his family had settled in, gave him mental relief from the worry that seemed to be a constant in everybody's lives. For several years now, the continuous discussion of what was right or wrong about slavery seemed to dominate all conversation. Searcy County scarcely had any slaves at all. The Bryant family, who came from Wayne County about the time everybody else did, owned two slaves.

Their farm was on Buffalo River, some 12 to 15 miles away from the communities along Big Creek and

Campbell. All travelers, whether they were passing through or whether it was more settlers, continued the discussion of the political battle that the country was engaged in.

Nathaniel had been right when he commented, "Zeke got his freedom, but this fight is far from over."

Noah returned from his walk below the spring still thinking about how he could solve the problem with the water spreading out over all the ledges and creating a hazard for livestock and children. His niece had fallen and broken her arm. It had not been set properly, and now her left arm hung crookedly, causing her hand to hang behind her when she walked. That was common in the 1850s when a broken bone was set by whomever was available to perform the task.

Noah's thoughts were confused. One minute he would be thinking of things in the present like how to redirect the spring water, in the next he would be trying to be clear in his mind on the issue of slavery.

Searcy County was not supportive of the South in their attempt to protect the right to own slaves. There were several families who considered themselves southern people.

Nathaniel sat on the porch of his house when all the Sitton clan gathered together and discussed what their position would be if it resulted in a split in the country.

They were conservative religious, moonshiners, farmers, and made their living working the land themselves without the benefit of slaves. At the same time they objected to the government sticking their nose into the people's business when slavery had been around as long as there was biblical history.

During all of these discussions the younger members of the families had expressed an unwillingness to engage in any military conflict.

In other communities throughout Searcy Country the general consensus was that slavery was something they would not defend.

While Noah's mind remained confused about the political discussions about the right or wrong position on slavery, his thoughts returned to how to redirect the flow of the spring.

A couple of days later he returned to the edge of the rock that made up the boundary for the stream of water flowing toward the bluff. He decided that by drilling holes at the right angle, he would be able to create a new channel. He envisioned being able to create a series of ponds which would provide water in all the areas next to the buildings housing the milk barn, mule lot, and where they kept the young heifers away from the breeding stock.

He walked some hundred yards along the perimeter of the fence separating each building. Redirecting the water flow this way would create a perfect water supply for animals, and at the same time eliminate the hazard of the slick rocks.

Nathaniel came to check on Noah when he heard a hammer pounding in the direction of the spring. "What on earth are you doing?" he asked.

Noah stood up and pointed in the direction of all the buildings to the south of the houses.

"I'm going to cut through the rock and send the water that away," he told Nathaniel.

"You're what?"

Noah began walking along the way he wanted the water to flow.

"After I cut the rock and start the water running this way, I can dig a ditch and place rocks along here." He pointed to the ground between the area he wanted to move the water to, and the slick ledge behind him.

"It'll work," Noah said. He went back, picked up the chisel and hammer, and once again worked on punching a hole in the limestone.

"All I can see is just a lot of hard work," Nathaniel

commented.

He walked around Noah and crossed the spring branch. Then he turned and looked back in the direction Noah described where the water would flow.

"It might work, at that," he concluded.

Nathaniel returned to his house, leaving Noah pounding on a rock chisel with a four-pound hammer.

Noah had drilled a hole less than 2 inches deep and 2 inches in diameter in a little over an hour. He stopped and calculated how many holes he would need to blast the new channel. It was going to take 10 or 12, and they needed to be over one foot deep.

"I may have bit off more than I can chew," he thought.

Then he decided he needed the distraction rather than continue worrying about slavery and who supported what.

Noah spent his days working the crops and drilling the holes. It had become quite a conversation among the Sitton clan about what he was going to try to do.

"When the holes are finished, I will go to Marshall and pick up some dynamite, and blast the channel for the water," he explained.

He had a plan to load the dynamite, cover it with dirt, and then set off the blast. He had no idea how much powder he should use, or how much danger there was in what he was doing. The Huckabees, Emma's parents, had experience in mining while they were in Kentucky, but he had not asked them to help. He had become a much talked about fellow for attempting to blast limestone. It was not common to do that in Arkansas.

The holes were finished. The dynamite had been loaded by the oldest Huckabee son. Nathaniel had taken over the project from Noah; he was convinced Noah had a good idea.

Changing the flow of the stream had become a major project for everyone in the Sitton family. They stood directly behind Nathaniel's house while they watched Eric

Huckabee set off the blast.

The idea of dirt over the dynamite was a good one. They also added several fenceposts and rails to the pile. No one wanted the explosion to get out of hand. It didn't.

They stood in amazement and watched the debris fall back down from the blast. They all watched as the Spring branch became blocked and the water began to flow as Noah had planned. They added to the debris and created a dam, sending all the water running along the path Noah intended.

Noah made one mistake. He had only completed the new ditch about 60 feet away from the blast. He never thought about the spring immediately flowing in the direction he wanted. Now he would have to contend with digging in water to complete the project.

The project was now a point of curiosity for neighbors as far away as Campbell community, and Ethan Massey, along with two of his brothers, showed up to inspect Noah's project.

It had been a year since they had spent any time talking. It wasn't long until the discussion turned to all the controversy over slavery.

Zeke's family was an integral part of the Campbell community, and there was no way any of his neighbors would support the Confederate States of America as they now called themselves throughout the South.

A freed slave, Zeke had lived almost 40 years in a community with an Indian wife, and had developed an extended family for several miles radius. No one was going to support slavery after knowing what good citizens the whole family had become.

Noah listened as Ethan explained his belief. Noah answered every question with one answer: "Me and my boys won't fight against our neighbors, but we won't support the Yankees."

While changing the flow of the spring could furnish a

diversion from the daily problems and discussions, it could not solve the problem of slavery. Slavery was an issue, and the solution dominated everybody's thoughts.

CHAPTER 20

Nathaniel looked at the cuts of wood stacked together above his worktable. He was about to start with a few to make enough shingles to repair the roofs of all the Sitton houses.

The year was 1862, some 10 years after he and Noah had returned from the trial where Zeke had gained his freedom. The years had been successful for farming and developing the land acquired by Noah. They had not worried about who owned what as far as ownership. Nathaniel's house sat on the property originally deeded to Noah and Emma Sitton. Emma's parents, the Huckabees, owned about the same amount of land just north of the Sitton property.

Nathaniel Sitton had three sons, the oldest being Noah, and the youngest being William. The middle son, Wesley, had never married and still lived with Nathaniel and his mother.

Nathaniel started making shingles. He stood the first cut

of wood up on the table and began splitting the shingles. They all had to be the same thickness or they could not be used for repairs. They also had to be split to the proper width to replace a missing or damaged shingle.

He rotated the cut of wood and inspected it for knots. A shingle could not have a knot. That was the reason for a lot of leaks in the roofs needing repair. Nathaniel liked splitting the red oak, but it wasn't as good for shingles as the white oak. He had tried cedar, red cedar, or as some people called it, Eastern cedar, for making shingles. They did make a good shingle.

Nathan hated the red color, and he didn't like the way cedar weathered out with some areas turning black while other areas tended to become yellow or white. He decided for Noah's house he would make red oak shingles.

Wesley was the only one of his sons that hadn't joined the Confederate Army. Noah had taken his two sons to Texas to join the Texas Infantry as cooks. He still did not want to take up arms, but when the recruiter came by, he agreed to join if he wouldn't have to stay in Arkansas where all of his family was, and if he could limit his duties to cooking. William had joined the Tennessee Regiment from Wayne County.

The Huckabee family was in total conflict. Nathaniel did not know which regiment their oldest son had joined in the Confederate Army. The middle son refused to join either side, and so far had stayed home and worked on the farm like Wesley. The conflict came when the youngest son left without telling anyone he had gone. They had no idea what he had done until he sent the note saying he was joining the army somewhere in Illinois.

Nathaniel had started to split the first cut of wood when Eric Huckabee walked up beside him.

"Making shingles?" Eric asked.

Nathaniel hit two more licks with the hammer before he answered. "Yeah."

They both sat silent after Nathaniel had split three slabs of wood that could be turned into shingles. Nathaniel checked those slabs for thickness and they were identical. They would be good shingles.

"I like the shine of that red oak after it is split," Nathaniel said as he looked at the three pieces he had set aside as good for shingles.

"It will dry a good color, and it's easy to split and nail on the rood," Eric commented. "We heard from Bob who joined that Illinois bunch," he said, not sounding very happy.

"He okay?" Nathaniel asked.

"Yeah, I guess," Eric answered. "All he could write us was the name of his outfit."

"We ain't heard a word from the boys in Texas," Nathaniel said referring to Noah and his sons.

"You heard about them marching all those folks to Little Rock?" Eric asked.

"No, what you talking about?"

"A recruiter for the CSA came by asking for volunteers over around Campbell," Eric began. "And when he didn't get anybody, I guess most of the people ran him off their property." Eric picked up a piece of wood and began to whittle with his knife.

Nathaniel knew better than to interrupt Eric, because he was known for long periods of silence during his storytelling.

"I guess they came back and arrested everybody they could gather up and took them to Little Rock with chains around their ankles, and locked together while they marched toward the South."

Eric stood up, placed his pocket knife back in his overall pocket, and walked toward the spring branch that had been created by the blast a few years earlier. He stepped across the stream and looked down the ditch that had turned into a fast-flowing stream. Noah had created ponds in each area below the below the buildings. The one at the horse lot had big rocks to keep the water from flowing into the corral. The lot for the heifers had a long, shallow pool almost a foot deep. The last pond was deep enough for fish. The Sitton family would bring fish from the stream, turn them loose in the pond, and had nets to catch them for frying as needed.

Eric admired all of this before he continued the discussion of the chain gang leaving Marshall on their way to Little Rock.

"Uncle Nate." Eric addressed Nathaniel with the name everybody had started using for Nathaniel because he was entering his eighth decade. "This has ruined us all." He referred to the chaos which has been created over the fight for slavery.

Nathaniel Sitton was still able to do a hard day's work. He could fill the mash barrels with grain and water, and add the right amount of sugar for making whiskey. He could kill fish with a pitch gig. He could still see well enough at 80 years old to course a bee. Coursing a bee is watching a honeybee get water, and then watching them in flight as they fly a couple of circles around the spring, and take off in a "bee line." The term was coined bee line because honeybees fly straight from the time they leave water, or wherever they are gathering nectar, back to their hive.

Nathaniel had learned the art as a boy in east Tennessee while spending time with his grandfather. They would sit by a spring of water and watch the bees until they could position themselves directly behind their flight and determine where they needed to move to pick up their flight line again. Nathaniel thought about how much patience it took to move in about 200 feet increments, tracing the flight of the bees each time until you arrived at the hive.

He remembered how when they found the bee tree, the bees would drop off the line and fly a circle around the tree before entering the hole, usually a limb that had broken off the tree and the knothole had rotted leaving an opening into the hollow tree for the bees to enter. There was a code among the settlers that if you found a beehive, you marked it by using a large X on two sides showing your claim for the hive.

Eric and Nathaniel had sat quietly while Nathaniel's mind returned to a day of his youth, a time when the worries were much less dangerous than this time of the "Southern Rebellion," as the Yankees called it, and the "Yankee Aggression," as the Southerners called it.

Eric left. He had not given enough details of the of the chain gang from Searcy County being marched to Little Rock to satisfy Nathaniel Sitton's curiosity.

"Me and Wesley are taking the buggy and going to town," Nathaniel said to himself as he gathered the tools for making shingles and returned them to the toolshed.

"We'll go tomorrow." He headed over to the buggy to make sure it would be ready to go the next morning.

CHAPTER 21

Nathaniel recalled the trip he had made with Noah almost ten years earlier when they went to observe the trial for the ownership of Zeke.

The battle over slavery had moved from the courtrooms to the battlefield.

Nathaniel visited with John Rhodes. John had received a couple of newspapers, one from St. Louis, and one from Nashville, Tennessee. They each had carried stories over the years as the controversy had grown. Nathaniel remembered listening intently when John read the story of the election Abraham Lincoln as president. He also read the newspaper containing the story of the first battle at Ft. Sumter, South Carolina.

It had all seemed so far away, but this morning as he and Wesley traveled to Marshall, he was worried it had made it to Searcy County.

Wesley sat up and pointed. "Pap, you see them riders leave the trail when we started up the hill?"

"Yep, I saw them," Nathaniel replied.

"They are back in the trees on our right watching us."

Wes retrieved the scattergun from the front of the buggy and laid it across his knees.

"Look another direction," Nathaniel said. "Ignore them." They continued to drive past the riders sitting on their horses some 50 yards back in the woods to the right.

"I've been seeing a lot of strange people riding along the creek past the house lately," Nathaniel commented.

"I heard they robbed some folks down at the mouth," Wes said, referring to the mouth of Big Creek where it joined the Buffalo River.

"There's no law anymore with this war going on," observed Nathaniel.

They rode quietly after passing the riders with no contact being made with them. When they got to Marshall, Nathaniel parked the wagon behind the hardware store, just like he always did when he came to pick up supplies. They walked through the hardware store. Hardly anyone was in the store. There was a worker stocking supplies for horses. Bridles, harnesses, and a rack of shoes for horses was being replenished. The clerk was posting entries into her book, and spoke up.

"Good morning." After a pause she added, "Mr. Sitton."

Nathaniel nodded as was his custom. He started to walk past her to the front sidewalk, where a group of men stood talking quietly.

"What brings you to town today, Nate?" She used the name that was gaining popularity among all the people Nathaniel knew.

Nathaniel realized he was acting differently today because, usually, he would stop and place an order before going past the counter where she was working.

"I come to town to pick up a few things, but I want to know what happened." He turned to face the store owner.

She knew what his question was about, and didn't need

any details to understand his curiosity.

"They arrested Kurt, the sheriff, and then they took him with them, with his badge still on his chest. And as they approached each house they arrested all the men." She stepped out from behind the counter and continued talking. "They left one young boy and the women and children at each house. They took everybody else."

"They didn't come by my place," said Nathaniel.

"That's because Noah and the boys have gone to Texas to fight for the rebels," she said, irritation showing in the tone of her voice.

Nathaniel had always been friends with the Hayes family who operated the hardware store. It bothered him that Edith, the owner, was irritated.

"Did they take any of your family?" he asked.

"They took my husband and his brother, you know, the one who bought Zeke's freedom." Edith Hayes had tears in her eyes. "It really got bad."

Nathaniel and Wes left the hardware store and walked around the town square. There were only older men and young boys scattered in small groups, talking quietly. Nathaniel tried to join the Blair family, but they looked at him with almost the same contempt the store owner had shown.

After attempting to talk to a few people, Nathaniel went back to the hardware store.

"Have you got any good nails for putting on shingles?" he asked.

Without the store owner answering, the boy stocking the supplies for horses, walked to the nail bins. "Here's all we got." He pointed in the bin.

Nathaniel bought five pounds of nails to repair the roofs. The nails he got were not what he needed. He now would have to drill holes before using them to keep them from splitting the shingles. They would have to do.

Nathaniel and Wesley began their ride back to Big

Creek. They hadn't spent more than an hour in Marshall. Usually they spent a couple of hours visiting before even considering looking for supplies. But after having tried to visit, Nathaniel still had no idea how many people had been arrested and taken to Little Rock.

"We didn't learn nothing," Nathaniel said. But he did know that the people were mad.

They made it back to the Sitton homestead before dark. Nathaniel and Wes didn't have any conversation about what they had seen or heard during the trip. Nathaniel worried about the riders they met on their way to town. He worried about what would become of the neighbors who were taken in chains to Little Rock.

The only thing he learned was one comment he had overheard: "Thirty of those people from Campbell, and that one who caused all the trouble," referring to Zeke. They were in the front of the chain gang.

He needed to get back to concentrating on making shingles and repairing the roofs.

Nathaniel walked by the stack of shingles neatly placed together according to size and thickness. He looked at Noah's roof, trying to decide which shingles needed replacing. Wes had gone up in the attic and stuck a straw through the holes, which now protruded from the roof.

There were a lot of shingles to be repaired and replaced. Wes arrived with a ladder and leaned it against the side of Noah's house.

"Pap, we start here?" Wes asked.

"Yeah." Nathaniel grunted and walked closer. He looked up at the roof. "Go up high. See that straw that's sticking through?" Nathaniel pointed to the spot where he wanted to start. "We'll replace that one first."

He returned to where the shingles were stacked. He picked up two shingles, trying to determine if they were the size he needed for the space he needed to replace.

"We gotta drill holes for the nails." Nathaniel brought

the little hand cranked auger and three tiny bits, hoping to be able to drill the size holes they needed. He picked up a couple of the nails and looked at them in disgust. "If we had only been able to get the right nails."

As was Wes's style, he just listened, and did not make a comment.

Nathaniel marked the shingles and picked up the drill, handing it to Wes. "Drill a hole at each mark," he instructed as he handed Wes the drill.

Nathaniel at his age could still do a lot of work, but his best ability was instructing his sons on how to do the things he could no longer physically accomplish. He would never climb the ladder. Once Wes had drilled the holes and started up the ladder with four shingles, Nathaniel began sorting other shingles, and actually started drilling some of the holes.

Wes knew what he was doing as far as replacing a wooden shingle. He was careful to remove the shingle that needed replaced, and he cleaned the lath prior to measuring the replacement shingle. After he determined the right shingle to use, he slid it into place and drove nails through the predrilled holes. It fit perfectly.

The replacement of the shingles was going better than expected. It was almost time for the noonday meal. Emma, Noah's wife, had been cooking, and the smell was almost too much for hungry men to bear.

They went to the back porch and using the dipper, poured water from the bucket into the wash basin. They were just beginning to wash their hands when they heard screaming.

"Daddy shot 'em!" Eric Huckabee's youngest daughter came running into the yard, crying. She had obviously run all the way from the Huckabee homestead to the spot where she now stood.

Emma went to her, held her, and asked, "He shot who, honey?"

"The men that come on their horses and tried to get in the house," she answered. Over the next few minutes, after asking several questions, the child calmed down enough to tell the story. There were three men laying in the Huckabee yard shot. She did not know if they were alive or dead. She did know one got away.

While Nathaniel and Emma questioned the young Huckabee girl, Wes had been busy hooking the mules to the wagon. They climbed on board and headed for the Huckabee homestead.

Nathaniel stood looking at the bodies lying in the yard, and he looked at the horses where Eric had tied them.

"I took the rifles and climbed into the barn loft when I saw them come riding up the creek," Eric said. He went on to tell how he had loaded four rifles, and was waiting behind the hay in the loft when the fellows rode into the yard. There had been reports of robberies, murders, and several things stolen by riders who either were known as Jayhawkers or Ruffians, depending on whether they were from Missouri or Kansas.

"I waited until they grabbed hold of Mama, and as soon as she got loose, I started shooting. One got away. I think he's wounded."

Nathaniel stood deep in thought as other neighbors joined them. They heard the ruckus and all the screaming, and came to investigate.

"I was in town yesterday. We don't have a sheriff." Nathaniel paused. "They marched Kurt off with the rest of them when they took the chain gang to Little Rock."

The neighbors all stood and talked quietly, trying to decide what they should do.

"Just get them out of my yard and away from my house!" Mrs. Huckabee solemnly commanded.

Wes turned the fellow over that was lying closest to the house. Everyone was surprised at how young the dead man was, just a boy, maybe 17 years old. Wes went through the young man's pockets and discovered he had a number of gold coins. The saddlebags still on the horses had not yet been searched.

It had been over two hours. The bodies had been loaded into the Huckabee wagon, but no determination had been made about a burial. As they stood, looking into the wagon, one of the Baker boys from up the hollow toward Big Flat, rode in leading a horse with a body draped over the saddle.

"This 'un made it to our place." Luke Baker climbed down, pointing to the body on the hose.

Eric walked over, looked at the body, turned and said, "That's the fourth 'un. He didn't get away."

They loaded the fourth body into the wagon with the other three. Eric Huckabee was not surprised the fella didn't get away. Eric was known as the best shot with a rifle of anybody in the area. He looked satisfied, knowing that he had hit his mark four times.

The bodies were buried in a sandy loam area, just barely above the high-water mark above Big Creek, some 300 yards north of the Huckabee homestead. They placed rocks over all four graves, but did not attempt to make any kind of marker. They stood silently for a moment after finishing the burial.

"This is a shame," Nathaniel said. He paused, then with a tremor in his voice said, "I hope none of our boys are in the ground somewhere else."

They returned and began the task of going through the saddlebags. They spread out a collection of coins, some gold bars, rings, and three silver cups. Mrs. Huckabee picked up one of the cups and burst out in tears.

"This is Lizzie's." She hugged the cup to her chest. "I know because Bert gave it to her for their wedding day while we were still in Wayne County.

She was talking about their old neighbors who had moved to Arkansas a few years later than the Huckabee and Sitton families. Bert and Lizzie Bryant had settled below the bluff across from the mouth of Bratton Creek. It was some three miles from where they stood.

Eric and Wes mounted the horses left by the men they had just buried, and rode in a hurry to the Bryant homestead.

It had been almost two weeks since Eric had shot the four men, and he and Wes had tried to determine how many people had been robbed before they got to the Huckabee farm. They had returned everything to the Bryant children after they had buried Bert and Lizzie Bryant. There was a 17-year-old girl and a 15-year old boy now responsible for raising two brothers and three sisters.

Nathaniel and Wes picked up where they left off with roof repairs. Their conversation was stoic, filled with regret and hatred for what was happening in Searcy County.

CHAPTER 22

"**I**'m tired," said Wes Sitton. He seldom complained, especially while working with his dad. It was several weeks after the shooting in the Huckabee yard.

Nathaniel wasn't sure what Wes meant when he said he was tired. Maybe he was talking about climbing up and down the ladder and replacing shingles. Maybe he was tired of hearing about all the troubles that seemed to be happening almost daily.

Nathaniel watched as Wes gathered up their tools and returned them to the toolshed. During the daytime Nathaniel and Wes worked while Noah's two youngest sons hid in the woods above and below the house with rifles in hand, ready to defend the Sitton homestead.

There were constant reports of murders, robberies, and people being harassed even after they had been robbed. If one band of thieves came through one week, there would be two different bands a week or so later.

There were usually 3 to 5 riders with one riding in first

to a homestead and asking for food or water. If the family tried to help, before they could do so, the yard would be full of riders demanding treasures.

"Wes, we are probably one of the poorest regions of Arkansas, and we have people coming through trying to rob us." Nathaniel's comment broke the silence after Wes had returned the tools to the shed. "Why would you try to rob somebody living on the banks of a creek with nothing but sycamore trees and gravel bars? It'd be different if we were mining gold or something."

The comment made sense to Wes. He finally answered, "Pap, everybody's too broke to buy 'shine."

The Sitton moonshine still, tucked away above a crack in the bluff that was almost impossible to find, had not produced a gallon of moonshine in over two years.

Nathaniel sat on the porch looking to the east toward Big Flat. Time had been good, partly. Kids had been born, families had grown in numbers. He looked across the creek at all the houses that had been built for the new members of the Sitton clan. Noah and his two boys, Nathaniel's grandsons, had been gone to Texas going on three years. Noah's mom hung on to the three letters that had found their way to Big Creek.

Noah had written that he was doing well. "There's plenty of beef to cook, and the soldiers in Texas love to eat." One of the letters began. He went on to explain that his boys actually did not have to go out with the patrol, but they had become his helpers preparing food in the mess hall. A tent stretched over three wagons that carried supplies for the Texas infantry. The Texans were well prepared for war. Noah also wrote that the veterans from the war of independence with Mexico were still young enough to fight in this new war.

It worried Nathaniel that Noah would write a letter basically reporting on the military operation in Texas without writing anything more than he had a lot of beef to cook, and his boys were working with him feeding the unit they had signed on with. While he watched the sun set, and darkness began to fill in the hollow toward the creek, he worried because there was no order in the country at all. He had not returned to Marshall in over a year. He began getting his supplies at the store in Big Flat. For some reason Big Flat had stayed virtually untouched from the Jayhawkers and the Ruffians.

Because the terrain was flat, all the farms developed around Big Flat provided good visibility. A rider would be visible long enough for the homesteaders to be prepared before they could get inside the yards. Along Big Creek the timber provided cover for people to ride unseen until they were actually on the premises. Nathaniel also thought how tough the Wallace family, the Treat family, and the Bakers, along with the McCoys were from Big Flat. They knew how to defend themselves. In the few reports he had received of any of the Jayhawkers attempting to rob the houses, they had been unsuccessful.

He remembered how disappointed Noah and Ethan were when they realized they would not be able to settle at the spot they remembered from their survey days. At the same time, there was a lot more wildlife and fish, and the little fertile fields along Big Creek grew the best corn, potatoes, and any other vegetables they wanted to plant. It seemed everybody had settled where they needed to be over the last 35 years.

John Rhodes had been very successful with his gristmill. People showed up every day and took up their station to guard the access to and from the mill. There had been reports of murders and all kinds of violence on Oxley Mountain above Campbell.

Nathaniel's thoughts left these problems. He was so glad that he would not have to split anymore shingles, and Wes would not have to climb the ladder tomorrow. The roofs were repaired.

The sounds of dogs running and barking filtered down the hollow along the Hickory Branch behind Nathaniel. It was the first time he had heard foxhounds running in a long time. The Holliman family from Rock Creek had good dogs, but hadn't hunted foxes in years.

"I wonder why they would be doing that now?" he asked aloud.

The chase seemed to be headed directly toward the house. The dogs stopped barking, and all was quiet until Wade Holliman spoke up. "It's me, Nathaniel."

Nathaniel and Wade were joined by all the young Sitton men, including Wes and three of Wade's boys. The boys ranged from 12 to 14 years old, young enough to not have to serve in either army, Union or Confederate, but old enough to carry a rifle and be out at night.

Wade reported someone had broken into a house on the Buffalo River, and he had turned his dogs loose to track them. They led him to the big spring, up Hickory Hollow, but they had lost the trail.

"Are you sure it was a man?" Nathaniel asked after hearing the story.

"Don't know," Wade answered. "I just know that when the Avey boy came into the yard, he had been following a blood trail from the horse the man was riding."

"I turned my best two hounds loose on the trail. They followed it all the way from my place to just up the holler from here," Wade said. "I have no idea what the man looked like or what his horse looked like, but how could he just disappear?"

All the people who had gathered during the course of the early evening eventually left without any answers about the man, or if it was a man, the dogs were chasing.

When Nathaniel woke the next morning, his irritation with the events from the night before had grown. He was getting tired at 83 years old of being bothered continuously with all the trouble brought on by the war of aggression or the war of rebellion, depending on which side you felt allegiance to.

He had gone along with nothing, refused to join the Arkansas infantry, or go to Texas. He understood not wanting to side with the Union, even though he did not support slavery. This controversy left him in the position of losing friends and being considered almost a traitor to both causes.

Nathaniel took the warm drink Emma, Noah's wife, had made from some concoction she'd come up with to substitute for coffee which had not been available since the war began.

"I love coffee. It would be worth it to get this war over just so I wouldn't have to drink this stuff," he said aloud as he poured the rest of it out of his cup.

His patience was about exhausted. It was time for this to end.

CHAPTER 23

Noah was returning home from Texas after three years of cooking and following the troops who seldom engaged in any kind of battle. The state of Texas still considered itself a nation separate and apart from the United States. From 1836 until 1845 they had operated as an independent state.

After problems with maintaining order, establishing a monetary system, and just general difficulties maintaining their government, they joined the Union. They became the seventh state to join the Confederacy after Sam Houston was defeated for governor.

Noah's decision to go to Texas was based on the fact he did not expect them to march north to engage in battles with the Union. This turned out to be true. There had been very little action other than marching to areas suspected of blockading shipping and receiving goods.

Noah decided to return to Arkansas after receiving letters about how bad the renegade groups of men robbing and killing people was in northern Arkansas . He went to his commander and asked for relief long enough to return home and deal with the problem.

"I've got to go," Noah told his commander, after he received the letter detailing his brother-in-law Eric's shooting of four men in his yard as they tried to rob the Huckabee homestead. Emma had not written any details other than "Eric shot three of them dead on the spot, and the fourth one died somewhere between here and Big Flat. One of the Baker boys brought him back draped across horse, dead."

It'd taken over a month before Noah received the letter, and he, along with his two sons had been riding horses and leading three pack mules for almost two weeks before they got to Little Rock and crossed the Arkansas River and began the trek north to Searcy County.

The sun was setting on Big Creek. Nathaniel had finished the chores and watched the darkness as it came up out of the hollow, following the sunshine as it began making its nightly journey to the tops of the hills. He always liked to watch the change to shadows along the creek while the sun still shined brightly on the top of the hill. He understood the earth's rotation, and liked to believe the earth was round, and the globe they bought for the Cedar Creek schoolhouse was accurate.

"I can't believe there are still flatlanders who believe the earth is flat and has four corners." Nathaniel accepted modern education in the 1830s that actually proved Columbus could have sailed to the Orient if he hadn't collided with North America.

The banks of Big Creek and the hollows that led to Big Flat were not cultural centers with people reading and studying the latest scientific findings. But time was moving slow, a lot slower after the start of the Civil War.

It made no difference what name you preferred. Civil War, War Between the States, the Southern Rebellion, or the Northern Aggression, it had interrupted the lives of everyone.

Nathaniel stood listening. He thought he heard someone coming on horses. He looked south toward the hills that were now in the shadows. He stood still and watched as the blue tick hounds stood and looked in the same direction, where he thought he heard the horses.

"Pap, we're home!" Noah yelled while they still lacked some 200 yards before coming around the bend of the creek and ready to climb through the gap of the bluff to where the Sitton houses were built.

Nathaniel couldn't believe what he heard. He started running toward the gap. He was standing there when he saw three men ride toward him. His grandsons had been 15 years old and 17 years old when they left for Texas. One had been clean shaven, the other barely needing to shave when they left.

Nathaniel looked at Noah. He had lost weight. He was no longer paunchy with a belly that seemed to make him look shorter. Of course, he was not wearing his usual overalls with suspenders. He had on pants with a belt. Nathaniel wondered where they had gotten those pants, and why they were not wearing the uniform of the CSA, or the Confederate States of America. Then he realized it was probably a good thing they were not dressed as rebel soldiers.

The Union army had captured Little Rock. He had heard the chain gang from Searcy County had been released. Some were inducted into the Union army, while others returned home to Marshall. Nathaniel had not gone to Marshall to see if Kurt, the sheriff, was back, or if the Hayes brothers had returned to their hardware store in Marshall and to their Mercantile at Leslie.

Noah got close enough to jump down and run to his father, Nathaniel, stopping just short for a couple of seconds. They stared at each other before embracing in a hug.

David and Samuel Sitton watched their dad, Noah, and Grandfather Nathaniel exchange hugs, something they had never seen two Sitton men do. Hugs were for girls and women. They had been taught that as young men.

They sat on the porch several hours until it got dark, and then returned to the porch after the supper Emma prepared for everyone. They hung a lantern on the porch. Noah wasn't sure who had gone to the Huckabee homestead, but it had turned into a family reunion that went on well into the night.

Stories were told of camping along the Red River in Texas, of traveling south along the Sabine, and all the places they had marched in Texas continually across the northeastern corner trying to make sure no one was able to invade or blockade Texas.

"Pap, I never got used to those Texans," Noah had said early in the conversation.

"How?" asked Nathaniel.

"I don't know, really," Noah replied, "it's just, really, it's just that you always taught me never to brag, and, well, those folks do it all the time."

That was enough talk about Texas and about the time they spent there. Nathaniel began to try to catch them up on how hard it had been to stay out of trouble with the Ruffians and the Jayhawkers, and the people who quit work and spent most of their time worrying about stuff that never happened.

"After Eric shot those folks…," Nathaniel stopped and thought before he continued, "we didn't do nothing for a while except watch for people, follow tracks, and try to stay safe. It's been bad. Now with you and the boys back, we can get back to work, and just one or two of us watch out for Jayhawkers."

Noah took a walk the next morning. He inspected the water project where they blasted the rock out and changed the flow of the stream to water the animals in all three lots.

He liked what he saw. The big rocks he had placed along the lower edge of the ditch held the water very well. There was watercress growing around the edges of the rocks, and the water was clear. It had been a good idea.

Normal is a continual change from what it was the day before, and after years the change was significant. The two young men, Noah's sons, had grown considerably, and now their faces were covered with full beards. Their eyes were tired. The Sitton's eyes were always small and beady and seemed to be hidden beneath their brows, sitting behind their full cheeks. As children they might have blonde hair, and their eyes might seem even bigger, but as they got older their hair was always a darker brown. It seemed like, as they matured, their eyes became sharp, focused, and not so wide open.

Noah remembered when he and Ethan Massey had left to go on the survey, Ethan had commented that every day they were gone Noah had changed in appearance. While he had been 17 years old, and they were gone just over three years, when he returned at age 20 he imagined he had gone through about the same amount of change as his sons did while they were in Texas. They left as boys; they returned as men.

Things began to change along Big Creek and toward Big Flat as the war came to a close. Nathaniel's health began to fail not long after Noah returned. They were never sure what caused Nathaniel's death. He had worked hard the day he died. He had eaten with Mrs. Sitton, and came over to Noah's to sit on the porch and visit. Noah got up and went in the house for something, and when he returned he found his dad slumped forward in the rocker.

When they realized Nathaniel's coffin would have to be bought from Marshall, one of those built by the Kirkendalls, Mr. Huckabee agreed to sell them the one he had made for himself. It sat on his porch, filled with black-eyed peas waiting for the winter. Mr. Huckabee hoped he would have time to replace it before he died.

Noah had no idea why they decided to take Nathaniel to the Rock Creek Cemetery some 5 ½ miles north of the Sitton homestead. The horse-drawn wagon rolled along slowly with several people walking behind, and a few people riding horses even further back.

Emma said it was because he had gone out there about a year ago to help dig a grave. He had talked about how hard and dry it was, and about how hard it was to dig. "It's like being put in a tomb," he said.

They had to finish digging the grave after they got there. Nathaniel was right. It was cut through solid rock held together by a little bit of red clay. The digging was finished, and the patriarch of the Sitton clan was placed in his final resting place at the Rock Creek Cemetery.

A few months after Nathaniel was buried, word came that Lincoln gave an address at Gettysburg. Lee surrendered with the Civil War coming to a close.

The summer of 1865 was a mixture of good things and bad. Depending on the side you were on during the war, determined who your friends were now. The Sitton clan was marked because Noah and his sons had gone to Texas with the rebels. The Huckabees were divided even at their own homestead because they had one son return from fighting with the Union, and another who had left and gone to Texas and, reportedly, on into Mexico after the war was over.

When Noah read an article in a newspaper from whatever city it happened to come from, the story was always the same. There were still scrimmages in the South. There were plantation owners who were trying to reclaim their property from the carpetbaggers, and from the slaves who had been given 40 acres and a mule on the same property they had worked as slaves.

Noah was proud that Arkansas didn't have slavery in Searcy County. While he had neighbors who had been good friends before he left to go to Texas, they might not speak to him or be as friendly as they had been, because they spent time in jail in Little Rock for refusing to join the Confederate Army. They still liked each other, but it was going to take time to heal.

The healing time was about to begin. All of the settlers who made the long trek from Tennessee to Arkansas were going to try to find the peace and quiet planned when they originally started out. They didn't get to settle at Big Flat, the place where Noah and Ethan had dreamed of coming. That land had been taken by the Wallace family, the Baker family, the Holt family, and many more who had beaten them to Arkansas back while they were trying to decide who was coming, and when.

Noah sat in the spot where his dad, Nathaniel, always sat and watched the shadows turn to night as the bright sun topped the hill before disappearing. He thought back on the life Nathaniel had lived since they came to Arkansas. There were good times, and there were bad times, but they had accomplished what they set out to do. They had roots in a place called Big Creek, in a town being built called Big Flat, six miles to the east.

They had moved on from Wayne County, Tennessee, to Arkansas. It was home.

CHAPTER 24

David Sitton, the youngest of Noah and Emma's sons, enjoyed his walk along the gravel bar of Big Creek in October 1878. He watched a water snake catch a minnow and return to a spot underneath the dirt bank below the bluffs. He saw a small mouth bass watching as the snake swam away with the minnow.

He had grown up swimming in the water hole he was looking across. He could see the shadows of leaves floating on top of the water. The shadows moved along the slick rock bottom and seemed to be moving faster than the leaves. He knew that was not possible. There were a number of flies riding on the leaves, and as he watched, a large mouth bass came up and swallowed a leaf with three flies on it. He wondered about that. He knew the bass enjoyed capturing anything that had life for food, but what would it do with the leaf?

David remembered his grandfather, Nathaniel. One of his earliest memories was taking the same walk with his grandfather. They would always start by going first to the lot with the young heifers, then the mule lot, and last the lot where the milk cow and the goats were kept. Then they would go down off the bluff to the hog pen and check the fence around it where it extended out into the Hickory Hollow for water.

He walked along the gravel bed of the Hickory Hollow branch and observed each of the puddles formed by the water flowing through the gravel. He remembered Nathaniel saying, "I had always wondered what happened to all the water from the wildcat spring and the other big springs along Hickory Hollow until we found out the spring hole was actually where they joined the creek.

It was 300 yards upstream from the mouth of the hollow. He continued his walk by crossing the creek twice to get to where he now stood looking into the hole of water.

He turned and started walking back towards the homestead. He crossed the cornfield. It was for popcorn, a special corn from seed given to the family three generations ago while they were in North Carolina. Also there was a large kernel white corn grown for hominy and cornmeal for bread, and last but not least, the dark yellow corn from seed given to Jim Campbell by his Indian wife some 60 years ago. It made a special type of patty similar to Johnny cakes, but a lot more flavorful.

David walked up through the crack in the bluff and reached the ledge that formed the bench land with its soft, sandy soil. It was where the potatoes had been grown every year since Noah had built the cabin.

The smell of supper being cooked reached him about halfway across the potato patch. He had been looking at the ground covered by the leaves of the turnips he had sown in August. The turnips were almost big enough to start cooking, but they would be too strong to eat the size they were now. They had already eaten several "messes" of turnip greens this fall.

As he got closer to the house, he was met by the three dogs he told to stay under the porch. They were from the bloodline of Ethan Massey's dog he brought from Wayne County,Tennessee. David had no idea how many generations of dogs were between the pups, he raised them since returning from Texas and the Civil War, and the one Ethan brought from Tennessee.

The first dog had markings of a black and tan along with the blue tick hound everybody preferred. The three dogs were about five years old, and had been a wedding gift to David and his new wife, Stacy Massey.

David remembered when he saw Stacy before he left for Texas. He had seen her one day at the grist mill on Cedar Creek. He knew her dad's name was Edward, and that he was a good friend of Noah's. He learned later that she was Ethan's granddaughter.

Stacy had really dark hair, and eyes to match. Her skin was a smooth, dark olive tan. Her jaw was not square; she did not have a round face. Her eyes sparkled and lit up when David spoke to her.

He thought of her the whole time he was in Texas, and when he returned to Arkansas he wondered if he would be able to meet her again. He was quick to follow Noah when he had suggested they go see Ethan after they returned from the war.

David understood some of the tension between the two friends, but he never understood why his dad refused to go along with the rest of the people around Campbell. He had gone to Texas as he was told.

When Noah and Ethan took their conversation some distance away from David and Stacy, they were left alone beneath an oak tree. They just began to talk when they heard laughter coming from the two old friends. David watched as Ethan gave Noah a hug before they sat down underneath the tree to continue their conversation. By the time the two friends ended their conversation, David had asked Stacy if he could come to see her in two weeks.

That was over five years ago.

The smell of the food got stronger as David entered the cabin. "What you cooking?" he asked Stacy.

"Just one of Grandma's recipes," she answered.

Stacy's grandmother was one of Jim Campbell's daughters. Her mother was an Osage Indian. One of Ethan's sons had married Jim Campbell's daughter, while his daughter had married John Rhodes' son who ran the gristmill. The Wayne County immigrants continued their tradition of marrying outside of their clans, but still making sure they stayed with the group from Tennessee.

David sat down and reached for the plate of Johnny cakes. His mother had made them from a Huckabee family recipe, and his grandmother Sitton had made them from a recipe of hers. Stacy used a combination of all the recipes, and added the things she had been taught by her mother.

David remembered Noah laughing when Ethan said, "I've learned a lot from that wife of Jim Campbell's about cooking."

He remembered Noah cooking in Texas for the Confederate Army, and trying one of the recipes Ethan told him about. They were beef rolls made by using the cornmeal flour in combination with spices and peppers to make a thin tortilla roll, and then filling them with a combination of beef and other meat mixed together. They were then deep fried to a golden brown in a pot, and served with potatoes.

Tonight's Johnny cakes had a combination of dried beef and pork mixed in with the batter. They had been fried on top of the stove to a golden brown.

David complimented Stacy. "These are great!" She was expecting their first child, and had difficulty cooking because of her morning sickness. Regardless of what she cooked David was going to be complimentary.

"Dad came by today," Stacy said, referring to Edward

Massey, Ethan's only son. She did not add any details.

"What was he doing here?" David asked as he reached for another Johnny cake.

"He came to say grandpa, Mr. Massey, is not feeling well." She referred to Ethan.

David had always wondered why Stacy called her grandpa Ethan, Mr. Massey. Most grandchildren just called them grandpa. He had asked her about that and she said her mother told her about the Osage tradition of referring to the elderly with the highest honor. The title of Mr. meant the same.

CHAPTER 25

Ethan Massey's funeral in the community of Campbell was well attended. It was the first time since before the Civil War that a large group of the descendants of Wayne County, Tennessee, attended an event.

The conversation stayed civil with no one mentioning the time they spent during the war, whether it was part of the chain gang imprisoned in Little Rock or the Sitton clan who had gone to Texas as cooks for the Confederacy.

David and Stacy were proud to pull up in their new buggy. David bought it while he was on a trip to Springfield, Missouri. He visited the new wagon works there with intentions of buying a wagon. He drove home with a buggy with lights and the best seats he'd ever seen to ride on.

The closest they came to being insulted at the funeral was when one of the Campbell boys commented, "There must be a lot of money in the 'shine business."

"What's he talking about?" Stacy asked as they pulled

over to the side with the new buggy.

David couldn't believe her question. Although he never explained about the days when he would take a load of corn or other supplies down Big Creek below the mouth of Bratton to the still. He just assumed she knew the Sitton clan always made moonshine liquor.

They stood behind everyone else during the funeral, and Stacy exchanged hugs with all of her cousins after it was over. David liked those people. He could see why his dad always remained such a good friend to Ethan all these years.

They were riding along in the buggy when Stacy brought up the subject of money again.

"You never answered my question. About the 'shine."

"Where did you think I got the money to order the new Singer sewing machine you wanted?" he asked.

"I thought the Huckabees were the ones who made the whiskey." She answered.

"They do," David said, "but Grandpa Huckabee always worked for Grandpa Nate." He answered without turning toward Stacy.

"It doesn't make any difference," Stacy finally replied. "I don't care where the money comes from. I just wanted one of those new sewing machines."

David thought about the finances related to the moonshine business. Takes a good manager to make whiskey. You can't drink. You got to hire someone who don't, and then sell it for cash to someone who does. He remembered Noah said that's what Nathaniel had taught him as a boy in Tennessee. They had brought the thumper keg and worm with them when they came to Arkansas.

The first time David had seen it in operation was a trip with grandpa Nate to check on the still to see if it had been bothered during the war. He never really understood why they had shut it down all those years. But they immediately began making 'shine again when the war was over.

His thoughts returned to what Stacy had said about the sewing machine. Big Flat had become the center of trade for the settlers along Big Creek. Stacy and his cousin's wife, Lara, would take the buggy and go to Big Flat to get supplies. It was safe.

For some reason, Big Flat had been untouched by the Jayhawkers and Ruffians during the war, and they had recovered very quickly when the war was over.

There were four new sewing machines in Big Flat. One was the $400 model made by Howe. David was just proud Stacy accepted the cheaper one. His new buggy had only cost $480.

They made the ride home without much further conversation. David had been lost in thought, trying to remember all the stories Noah told about his and Ethan's adventures. He could remember the stories about how as boys they had marched with Col. Jackson to New Orleans. He remembered the stories about when they did the survey of Arkansas and planned their trip to settle at Big Flat.

He also remembered how Nathaniel would tell Noah how much better it was to be on the banks of Big Creek with fish and swimming within 100 yards, ready for dinner. And with vegetable gardens scattered around on the bench land, and the fertile bottoms for growing corn to make the 'shine.

He couldn't relate to their conversation, because having been born in the cabin Noah built on the banks of Big Creek, he couldn't imagine waking up somewhere else and calling it home. When he brought Stacy home after they were married, he saw the gleam in her eyes as he explained why each part of the Sitton homestead was built.

David set the box containing the sewing machine in the middle of the front room floor.

Stacy started the un-crating when she found the instruction manual. She sat in Noah's rocker on the front porch and started reading the instructions. "I'm so glad

Grandma Massey taught us to read," she said aloud as she looked at the pages of the instructional manual.

She remembered the day her grandmother handed her a slate and a piece of chalk. She recalled how they spent days working from a book she was never allowed to touch, but was used to instruct her how to create letters and to read from the book.

Her grandmother would write words on a chalkboard that had been attached beside the fireplace, and was next to a window which provided light. She had no idea how long they had been studying with that one book, when one day her grandfather, Ethan Massey, walked in and said, "Look what I've got!" He held up a copy of McGuffey's Reader.

Stacy walked back to her cabin clutching the new book in both hands in front of her. She remembered lying on the floor trying to read until her mother made her stop.

She continued reading the instructions for assembling and operating a Singer Sewing Machine. Her mind wandered to her other grandmother, an Indian who married Jim Campbell. Emma loved hearing her Grandfather Jim tell the story of how he and Zeke met their wives.

Two Indian maidens, traveling with a small band of Indians from Kansas, became separated from their tribe when a different tribe attacked. The girls, about 15 years old at the time, ran into the woods and hid underneath a bluff until the next morning. For several days they had been lost, and had not encountered any sign of another human being.

Then, just before dark, they heard sounds of chopping. When they got closer, they saw Jim Campbell, a white man, along with the first colored person they had ever seen.

"Zeke!" Jim had yelled, and Zeke returned to stand alongside Jim.

The four of them stood staring at each other. Stacy's grandmother laughed whenever she told the story.

"We couldn't speak a word of understanding to each

other," she said. "But, for some reason, we were not afraid of them."

Zeke came closer to them first, and began gesturing, trying to communicate. Again, Stacy's grandmother would burst into laughter when she told the story.

"Here we are, two Indian girls lost in the woods for we didn't know how long, and we were being talked to in a language neither of us understood, but there was a thrill when we found other life." She would tell the story with tears in her eyes.

"I have no idea how long it took for us to start communicating." She would pause, then say, "I just knew that I belonged to Jim, and my sister belonged to Zeke. She would go on to say that she didn't remember how much time passed before Jim and Zeke decided to take them and settle in the area where they eventually built cabins. She did say, "Zeke tried so hard to teach both of us their language, while Jim was trying to decide what we were going to do.

"Before we ever got our first cabin built, we were both expecting a child." Stacy's grandmother would tell this just matter of fact, without any expression of guilt or pride.

She had loved hearing the stories from her mother and grandmother. A not so fond memory was the period of time when everyone worried that Zeke was going to lose his freedom. Stacy couldn't remember any discussion of the difference in color of her uncle or her cousins. She wasn't sure if they just accepted it without realizing there was a difference, or what.

David joined her on the porch, she was sitting in the rocker that belonged to his mother.

"You making much progress on getting the sewing machine set up?" he asked.

She didn't mention any of the thoughts she let wander through her mind while she was reading the manual. She couldn't explain why they interrupted her while she was reading the manual. They brought back a lot of memories. She realized how important it was for her grandmother Massey to teach all the children around Campbell community to read.

"If you will put it together, I will read the instructions and you can do the work," Stacy said.

With the plan for the assembly in place, they finished the job by the light of the new kerosene lamp David had bought in Springfield, Missouri, when he bought the buggy.

David woke up the next morning to the sound of a Singer Sewing Machine. Stacy had successfully started the first garment for their expected new resident.

CHAPTER 26

David Sitton rode one of the horses belonging to the youngest of the men his uncle Eric Huckabee had shot. He looked at the overgrown, unkempt spot in the corner of the field below the Huckabee homestead.

He was in Texas when the shooting occurred. He had listened to several stories about the incident since he got home. He looked at the bridle where it crossed the horse's head, and admired the little stamp on it indicating it was made in a leather shop in Denver, Colorado.

When Eric gave him the horse and saddle he said that no one had ever shown up claiming to know any of the four fellows. When he looked at the number on the flap of the saddle, he was fascinated that someone with this quality of equipment would be out committing crimes. When he tried to imagine where the young man was from, he always came up with western Kansas or eastern Colorado because of the saddle and bridle. He knew the horse was a quality breed, and showed signs of some thoroughbred, along with the

Arabian horse, a breed which a lot of people preferred.

He rode past the grave which contained the four bodies. One year a groundhog had made its burrow into the grave, but the burrow was not discovered until the following winter. David thought how sad it was for this young man to have wasted his life and then have his final resting place invaded by a groundhog.

"I don't feel a bit of sympathy for them, because they killed Lizzie," his grandmother Huckabee said one night after supper while they took a walk down to where the guys were buried.

"I've still got that...," Eric paused, then added, "thing I've told anybody they could have if they could identify it."

"What was he talking about?" David asked Noah, after they returned from the walk.

"I don't know," Noah answered, then went on to say it was something valuable, but they were not going to give it to anyone until they could tell them what it was and describe it.

David guessed, along with everyone else, but Eric had insisted he was not telling anyone, even in the family, because if anyone ever showed up and could tell him exactly what the men had on them, he would give them their property.

Noah and Emma, David's mother, would laugh, and talk about the people who come by and claimed to have lost everything imaginable, hoping to guess what it was.

David rode along the banks of Big Creek. He was on his way to the moonshine still. His brother, Sam, had worked at the still ever since they'd gotten back from Texas. David seldom went near it, but he was in charge of finding new markets. There was a lot of whiskey being made now that the Civil War had ended. They sold their highest quality 'shine to a buyer in St. Louis.

Sitton liquor, as the St. Louis buyer preferred to call it, was the highest quality moonshine he had ever seen. David imagined it was a result of grandpa Nathaniel being able to decide the quality of the corn, the wheat shorts, the starter cake for fermentation, and the exact amount of sugar.

Noah had said, "It's the water from that spring."

They had built a sluice out of a cedar log that carried the water from inside the cave out to a barrel. No insects or anything ever got in the water. They made sure that an exact amount of water was placed in each barrel prior to adding all the ingredients.

Although Nathaniel Sitton had been gone several years, his instructions were followed every day exactly the way he had given them.

David's ride, while he was thinking about the moonshine business, had taken him to the place where Bratton Creek joined Big Creek. He stopped his horse and faced the mountain to the east while he listened for other riders. Another one of Nathaniel's instructions. "Don't ever ride up to the still without stopping and making sure no one has seen you or can follow you to it."

Those words still echoed in every one of the Sitton family's minds as they tried to protect their moonshine business.

David rode up through the crevice. He was at the still.

The fire under the thumper keg glowed with bright red embers, emitting very little smoke.

"Grandpa Nate would be thrilled," David said as he walked up to Sam, pointing at the fire.

"He wouldn't have been really proud of us this morning when we stopped up the worm and almost blew the place up," Sam answered. He walked around and pointed to the relief valve that Noah had come up with.

It was a copper fitting that Noah had screwed into the side of the thumper. It had a plug made of wood which would blow out if the pressure got too great. This little gadget had prevented an explosion where the worm fastened to the top of the thumper.

Over close to Sylamore two fellows had been scalded really badly. It was hard to explain to everyone what they were doing when they got burned.

David stood, watching. "You making one runs?" he asked. The name they had given to 'shine that was lower in quality and alcohol than the product they shipped to St. Louis.

"Yeah, it's for Eric to sell out of his barn," Sam answered.

It was the first time David realized that their uncle Eric Huckabee was peddling 'shine out of his barn.

Emma, the boy's mother, had always insisted that the Huckabees did not make 'shine.

"We are good, honest folk, and we don't mess with moonshine," was the line she always used any time Noah started to criticize any of the Huckabee clan. Noah could not believe that she didn't know that her family had worked for the Sittons making moonshine for three generations. It was why they always lived in the same area, and stayed together each time they moved. He would just let it drop. Let his wife believe whatever she chose to believe. That was the best way to get along.

David left the still. He really hadn't had a good reason for coming today. He had enjoyed the ride along Big Creek, and really appreciated the quality of the horse he had ridden. He usually didn't give much thought to the young man who had ridden into the Huckabee yard and had been killed shortly thereafter. Today was different. Maybe riding by the spot where the men were buried had caused him to think about the horse's original owner.

As he rode back up the creek, he looked at the rocks in each of the bigger holes of water. It was these rocks that caused the holes of water to form. When the creek flooded, the rocks held the flow back long enough for the water to erode deeper holes.

He watched as a smallmouth bass chased a minnow until

it was in the shallow water, it was half out of the water before it returned back to the deeper pool. He wondered if the four riders Eric shot had looked at the streams they rode along. Or were they preoccupied with the treasures they were taking from the settlers along Big Creek?

He always believed when he got back from Texas and heard the stories about the Jayhawkers and Ruffians who raided this area, the reason was no organized resistance. The sheriff for Searcy County had spent that time locked up in Little Rock by the Confederate government because he would not join the southern army. It left these people vulnerable. They were in a land too rough and rugged for an army to march across, there was no reason to defend the area. There was absolutely nothing to be gained by controlling the hills around Big Flat and along Big Creek during the war.

David put the saddle in the tack room. He dumped grain in the feed bin for his horse, and began the long process of currying and brushing him down. David enjoyed doing this most of the time, and usually the horse showed his appreciation by wallowing in the lot as soon as he finished the grain.

David walked slowly to the house. He wondered how long Stacy had sewed on her new machine while he was gone. When he opened the door, his rocker had a new garment hanging across the back. He picked it up. It was easy to tell that the new resident, who should be born shortly, was the intended owner.

He startled Stacy when he walked into the kitchen. She was just beginning to cook their supper.

"I lost track of time sewing, and supper is going to be late," she said when she turned and looked at David.

He didn't answer. He just gave her a kiss on the cheek, and went to the back porch, where the wash basin sat, to clean up and get ready for a meal that would be late with a good reason.

CHAPTER 27

David watched as William Henry Sitton tried to throw a rope on the young horse. He would never forget the morning Stacy woke him and told him she believed it was time for the baby to be born.

When David's mother, Emma, and Eric Huckabee's wife had completed the delivery, they asked David to come in and meet his new son. David stood in awe, looking down at the best- looking little guy he had ever seen.

There were several visitors and many discussions during the next few days, but a name had not yet been chosen. David objected to naming the baby William, because he was sure he would grow up being called Willie. That was a name David didn't particularly like. But he had given in, and in the last couple of years William Henry Sitton became Willie.

Willie was a natural at everything he tried to do. David wondered if Willie could handle the colt he was trying to rope, and just about then Willie successfully lassoed the colt. David watched as Willie set his heels and stepped forward slowly until he was able to grab the pony's mane.

It had been over 13 years since Willie was born. This period after the war was called Reconstruction, the name generally used by everyone across the nation. David had witnessed a lot of change along Big Creek. Homesteads had been deserted. There had been new ones tried. The ones with good water and good land survived.

The Sitton family had done well financially. They bought homesteads as soon as the owners decided they could not make it, and they now owned a lot of land in the hills on each side of Big Creek. They hired people to come in and live in the old cabins, and these people now worked on a percentage basis harvesting timber. They cut oak trees and hued out cross ties for the railroads. They hewed the cross ties, by hand with a broad axe, they were good enough quality the railroads were buying them.

Every time a wagon load of cross ties left the Sitton property, they were paid roughly $20 in gold. Even after they split the money, there was still a lot of profit to the Sitton families. There were some 20 families living on the property they had acquired, and were working basically as sharecroppers.

The system fell into place after the Civil War set the slaves free, and they became sharecroppers for their previous masters. David wondered how Noah Sitton was able to do what he had done, but he was proud of their success.

He went to the corral and asked Willie, "Son, would you want to go on a trip with your dad?"

"Where?" asked Willie.

"We'll take the buggy and go to West Plains, Missouri."

"Why are we going there?"

"To find out about where that horse Eric gave me came from," David answered.

They left early in the morning. They crossed the White

River at about the same place the Sitton and Massey families had crossed years earlier. They made it to Old Joe, just south of Norfork, and they stopped to spend the night. They had planned on staying in a tent they carried in the buggy, but the trading post owner had asked them to spend the night with him.

"Your family name is Sitton?" the trading post operator asked.

"Yep," David answered.

"My family was here when you all camped for a while before going on across the river," he said. "My name is Cox."

"From Tennessee?" David asked.

"Yeah, just east of Wayne County."

David and Willie bedded down in the bunk room. It was obvious charging two dollars per bed was making good money for the trading post. It was clean, but it was also obviously for men only passing through. There were no facilities to provide for families to spend the night, especially women.

David thought about all the stories he heard about when the settlers came to Arkansas. He heard his grandfather Nathaniel talk about while they were at Old Joe. He had looked around at the land, trying to decide if they wanted to homestead there. David remembered him telling the story about finding a pile of broken plow points. After he had walked through the limestone glades, he realized the soil was not deep enough to plow. After all these years there still were not any homesteads along the glade stretch north of White River between Old Joe and Calico Rock.

They left early the next morning and continued their journey north toward West Plains. The terrain changed shortly after getting into Missouri. David also remembered his grandfather Nate saying several times after they settled on Big Creek, "I wish we had checked out the land more when we came to that big junction in the trails in

Missouri." That junction was now West Plains, where the trails split with some going further north into Missouri and others heading west. They had taken the one south toward the White River because of Ethan and Noah's dream of settling at Big Flat.

During the ride in the buggy from Old Joe to West Plains, they mostly discussed things of the past. Willie never seemed to run out of questions. David told almost every story he heard about things that happened while Nathaniel Sitton's family were camped at Old Joe. He remembered the stories of people going to Big Flat, the place Noah dreamed about settling, and he heard about the Wallace family who arrived years earlier and established a trading post. He remembered his dad, Noah, constantly complaining that the time to leave Wayne County was always delayed by one excuse or another.

He told Willie the same stories his grandfather and dad told about how difficult it was to cross the Mississippi River. Some 60 years later those problems had been solved, and it was easy to cross either by ferry or a railroad bridge where a section was built underneath the tracks for wagons and buggies to cross on the same bridge.

They were heading to West Plains to check out a train which would take them 'most anywhere they needed to go. His goal was to find out the origin of the horse that Eric had given him when he returned from Texas. He had read everything he could find about the bloodline of the horse, and all the stories led eventually to a ranch in Colorado.

David's mind wandered as he looked at the land they were passing through, and he thought about the turmoil of the last few years. The period after the Civil War ended was chaotic. After Lincoln's assassination, the restoration of the union had been difficult for all of the country.

David believed the area around Big Flat and along Big Creek had not suffered as much as areas where more government was in place before the war. He had heard stories of fights almost every week brought on by discussion of things that needed to be forgotten and left in the past.

After the first election following the war, in 1868, the confusion had spread all over Arkansas. David considered joining the Ku Klux Klan. The only reason for doing that around Big Flat and along the Buffalo River and its tributaries was to be able to stop the crimes being committed because the local government had broken down.

He didn't consider it in the same tone as the organization was throughout the South. He was not prejudice against slaves and their freedom. But he felt a need to join with his neighbors to be able to maintain order, and to protect their interests. He knew if he decided to join, Noah and his dad would join with him. It would not be a secret society in Searcy and Baxter counties. They might still wear the white robes and hoods, just for effect.

He continued driving the buggy. Willie decided to lean back and take a nap, but he continued wondering about the things that occurred in the last few years.

The most recent story he heard at Big Flat was when a veteran of the Union Army had come to the Post Office to pick up his mail. It contained the third Treasurer envelope that had come through the Post Office in the last two months. When the Postmaster handed the envelope to the veteran, he asked, "Mr. Pemberton, why are you getting a government pension?"

Charles A. Pemberton was the great grandfather of this author, Sam Pemberton. He fought the first three years with the South, under the leadership of a distant cousin, General John Clifford Pemberton. He had been disciplined rather severely at Vicksburg, and rather than submit to the punishment, he deserted and went to Dover, Arkansas. In 1863 he joined the Union Army and was stationed in North Little Rock at Camp Robinson. He had become acquainted with several of the Searcy County prisoners who objected to the Confederate Army and had been put in the stockade. Note that this particular paragraph is the only departure from being a pure novel. Please disregard any effect it may have on the rest of the story.

Instead of answering the postmaster directly, Mr. Pemberton went into a tirade about how he could get a pension from either side of the war. He had defended the South for three years and then switched to the Union. He had been honorably discharged from one, while the other one wanted to imprison him.

This was one example of how the war affected relationships over the last few years.

"Son, there's some really good-looking farmland along here," David said as they passed the farms just south and west of their destination.

Willie, awakening from his nap, slowly turned his head. He observed the red short horns grazing in the pasture south of the trail.

They passed a horse very similar to the one Eric had given David.

"That horse looks like yours," Willie said.

"We will stop at the farmhouse and ask some questions," David said.

They pulled the buggy up to the hitching post. They were still some distance from the front veranda of the fairly newly built house. A couple of dogs approached them. They were not hunting dogs. They were dogs bred for handling livestock, showing this farmer's priority to take care of the herd of cattle they passed, along with the horses they saw in the corral.

"Where you folks going?" the farmer asked as he stepped down off the porch.

"We're headed to West Plains, but we passed a horse back there that I would like to ask you some questions about. We have one very similar," David said. He walked toward the man and stuck out his hand in greeting.

"You mean the Arabian with a bit of thoroughbred showing? I got him from a guy who bought them from a ranch in Colorado," he said.

A few minutes later David said, "We've got to be going. We want to try to get to West Plains before dark." He shook the farmer's hand.

The man from whom the farmer purchased the horse from lived two blocks from the train depot in West Plains. They checked the buggy and horse into the livery stable, and walked to the hotel. West Plains was a booming town. There were travelers everywhere. They got to town in time to hear the evening train blow its whistle as it pulled away from the depot.

Willie had never seen anything like it before. The largest piece of equipment he ever saw picked up speed. Black smoke roiled from the smokestack of the engine. The wheels clacked loudly on the rails. All the horses nearby panicked. David was proud theirs were in the livery being fed grain.

They located the man easily who bought the horse in Colorado and sold it to the farmer. He gave them the name and location of the ranch just west of Denver.

David and Willie finished breakfast at the hotel. They walked toward the train depot.

"Where are we going?" asked Willie.

"I want to see the train schedule, and how we would make connections to get to Denver, Colorado," David replied.

Two hours later they boarded another train headed to Springfield, Missouri, and on to Wichita, Kansas. David paid the livery stable to keep the buggy and horse while they were on their trip. He went to the Post Office and sent a note back home to Stacy telling her they were going to a ranch in Colorado and buy horses. He ended the note by saying, "I will send a letter from Colorado and tell you when to have somebody, preferably my Uncle Eric, meet us in West Plains when we return."

Several days later they reached the depot just west of Denver in Golden, Colorado. They asked the ticket agent how to get to the ranch. Before he could reply, a fellow behind them said, "I can take you there. I work on that ranch. I came to meet the train and pick up supplies. You can ride with me''.

Soon they climbed on the wagon, and were on their way to the ranch headquarters. David was amazed by the mountains surrounding the beautiful valley and the ranch headquarters. He stared at the snow-covered mountains to the west. He looked at the different bands of timber covering the mountains, and the evergreens growing up next to the snow. He had no idea about the birch and poplar and other trees growing further down in the valley.

David and Willie were special guests in the ranch house, and Willie could not believe the size of the house. They were told the history of how the ranch came into being. It was funded by a family from England. The manager had not been an owner in the beginning, but was now buying the ranch through a contract which guaranteed the original owner a percentage for many years to come as payment for their investment.

David didn't ask any questions. He was here to check out horses, and after the tour and all the explanations about the origins of the ranch, they finally stood by a corral that had probably 25 horses eating from the trough that split the corral into two areas.

David spotted a horse that looked to be the same age and size as the one Eric had given him, the one ridden by the young man buried on the bank of Big Creek.

"Tell me something about that horse," he said, pointing.

"We had two of those," the rancher began. "I gave one to each of my sons." The rancher paused, looking toward the mountains in the west. Tears filled the old man's eyes. He turned back and once again looked at the horses.

"I don't know what happened to my youngest son, or to the horse I gave him." He walked over to the corral and leaned on the top rail, crossing his arms. He placed a boot on the lowest rail of the corral fence.

This can't be true. David stood quietly, waiting.

"He left here sometime during the 1860s," continued the rancher. "We were buying stock wherever we could find them, trying to build a herd. We heard there was some good cattle in south Missouri. He left here heading there to buy cattle."

Willie was so interested in all the things he had never seen before, he lagged behind and wasn't really listening to his dad and the rancher. There seemed to be 50 people working in the area around the ranch headquarters. There were barns for cattle. Haystacks rose neatly between all the buildings, stacked outside without any protection. As he came closer to the haystacks, he could smell the alfalfa. The Sitton family had tried unsuccessfully for years to grow alfalfa on Big Creek.

Willie caught up with his father and the rancher in time to hear his dad ask, "Is there anything you can tell me about your son who left that would help me know where he is?"

The rancher gave many details. He described the saddles and bridles he had bought his sons when he gave them the horses. "He was carrying a lot of money in a special money belt," he added.

David's mind raced. He thought of the secret Eric was keeping about the item he had which no one was ever able to come close to identifying. But why would a boy on the best horse they had ever seen, with a lot of money strapped on him to buy cattle, get mixed up with three thugs, Jayhawkers, and wind up getting killed in Arkansas?

David and Willie spent three days deciding on the horses they wanted, and then decided to buy two heifers and a bull to take back. They left the ranch assisted by four ranch hands. David rode in the buggy with Mr. Reynolds, the ranch owner. They had established a friendship.

It bothered David to listen to the man mourn his son. David was sure from all the stories that Mr. Reynold's son was the young man buried on the bank of Big Creek.

David took with him an envelope full of information about the breeding of the horses they bought, as well as the cattle. It was stashed away, ready for the trip by train back to West Plains. He would not stop thinking about all he had learned until he was able to sit down with his uncle Eric Huckabee and tell him the most unbelievable story he had ever heard.

Four days later they unloaded the cattle into the lots at the train depot in West Plains. They saw no sign of Eric, or anyone else from the Sitton homestead, to help them drive the livestock home.

CHAPTER 28

Willie sat on the bench on the livestock side of the railroad depot. He looked at the horses they brought back from Colorado in one corral, and the bull and two heifers in the next one.

They had been fed and watered before he got out of bed at the hotel. David had let him sleep, not bothering to let him know where he was going. Willie went to the railroad depot because that was where they would leave from to go back to Big Creek.

There was no sign of Eric and the two people who were supposed to meet them in West Plains.

Willie knew it was not Eric Huckabee's fault. David told him it would probably take seven or eight days for them to make it back to West Plains with the livestock. Everything had gone perfectly. They had stopped for two nights, put the livestock in a corral for feeding and watering. The rest of the time the train traveled without any problems or anything to slow it down.

While he sat trying to remember all the things he had done on his trip to Colorado, he was overwhelmed. Not quite 14 years old, and he had been brought out to a world dominated by men. He remembered the cussing and tobacco chewing throughout the whole trip.

He thought back to when his mother, Stacy, insisted on reading the entire Bible to him when he turned 12 years old. He wasn't sure how long it had taken. He remembered after she had read the first two chapters, she had asked him questions. He had not listened well enough to answer. She read them again. From that point on he paid attention.

He remembered when they finished. They stood up. Stacy looked down into his face, and in a serious voice said, "Son, I don't expect you to remember the entire Bible, but I've read it to you because it will measure and guide you through your life." Using the galluses of his overalls, she pulled him closer and gave him a hug.

"Promise me three things. The Sitton family has always made moonshine. Don't ever drink to the point of becoming drunk." She pushed him back to where she could look at him in his entirety. She was silent for quite some time before she continued. "The second promise is don't ever take up that nasty habit of chewing tobacco."

Then she made him promise the last thing. "Don't ever cuss."

Willie had promised.

Now he was getting older and finding it harder to keep the last one not to cuss since he was bullied on the schoolyard because he was short.

According to the marks on the porch indicating Willie's height as he had grown, he hadn't grown any in the last year and a half. He was stuck just short of 5'8". It really didn't bother him to be short. He was able to hold his own in a scrap by getting inside the long-armed fellows and giving them a squeeze they couldn't tolerate. He had heard them yell "calf rope" a lot of times, the signal throughout

Big Creek that anyone had enough of a fight. Willie was good at getting people to holler "calf rope."

Willie's mind wandered back to Colorado. He had enjoyed the time immensely. He spent most of the days riding with younger cowboys to feed hay to the cattle in various pastures. He enjoyed watching how they could handle those bales of hay with a hay hook, and how they jerked the wires off as soon as the bales hit the ground, kicking them around for the cattle to eat. He admired their use of horses and roping and branding a couple of calves. They hadn't branded any cattle on Big Creek. Everybody knew what was theirs, and you didn't try to take other people's stuff along Big Creek in Searcy County.

David and Mr. Reynolds spent several hours as David decided what he wanted to do about buying horses. Finally, Mr. Reynolds picked out one of the Arabian crossbreds very similar to the horse Eric had given him.

Willie didn't understand all that gone on while Mr. Reynolds and his dad had been together. But during the train ride back to Missouri he watched as his dad become silent and pensive. He knew it had something to do with the horse Eric had given his dad.

David returned to the dock and sat down by Willie.

"I found a team of mules and a wagon that we can haul the bull back to Big Creek. I think we can put everything we bought in the buggy, and you can drive it and lead the horses behind the buggy." David had planned how they would start back to Big Creek if no one showed up to help them with the stock.

"We'll just have to put halters on the two heifers and lead them behind the wagon and the bull." David stood up and they started toward the hotel. "Let's go get something to eat," he said.

David stepped down off the railroad depot and waited while a wagon hauling hay passed in front of him. The people who ran the stockyards were feeding the cattle being held before being shipped from West Plains, Missouri.

They ate in silence, with no mention of any of the happenings during the trip. David did not mention any of the conversation he had with the ranch owner. Willie sat, trying to digest all the things he had done. He had insisted on three pair of Levis that were sold in the store where they bought three saddles, two bridles, saddle blankets, and a lot of other supplies. He had even gotten a belt to wear with his Levis, just like the cowboys he had spent the last few days with feeding cattle.

He wondered what his mother was going to say when she saw the pants with legs six inches longer than his legs, and the cowboy boots he had insisted on having. The pant legs would barely go over them when he wore them. If she ever got the pants adjusted.

Sometime during the night Eric arrived with a wagon and two of his boys to help with the return to Big Creek. Eric ate breakfast at a separate table with David, while Willie sat with his two second cousins who constantly asked questions about everything in Colorado.

He couldn't help but watch as David explained something very serious to Eric. Willie knew it had something to do with the boy who was buried in the mound of dirt at the end of the field. He knew it had to do with whatever Eric had held all these years in secret until someone could identify it. He knew enough to be curious. He listened as much as he thought they would tolerate, but there was a lot left to be learned about the things they found out in Colorado.

They finished breakfast and spent over two hours getting together the caravan of wagons, a buggy, and two horses, along with two heifers, that were going to have to walk back to Big Creek.

"Eric we'll camp at Old Joe," David said, "but it will probably take us two days to get there. I don't know where we will find ourselves tonight."

They basically followed the same trail back to Big Creek that their families had followed several decades previously when they came from Tennessee.

CHAPTER 29

Stacy sat by the window trying to sew a seam up the leg of the Levis David had bought Willie while they were on their trip to Colorado. The Singer sewing machine she'd had for 14 years still worked great. But sewing the legs of the heavy denim turned wrong side out to make them fit over Willie's boots was a problem. She first had to shorten them to an acceptable length for Willie, but when he put the pants on over the boots he didn't like the way it looked. Stacy was disgusted.

"Willie, come in here," she called.

Willie sat on the front steps of the porch listening to the sewing machine. He was trying to figure out if he was going to attempt to ride the new horse again. He had spent the last three weeks since they had come home mostly in the corral. He finally got up and went inside.

"Try this pair on, "Stacy said, "I don't want to do anything else until I'm sure we are getting it the way you want it."

Willie took the pants and went to his room. He tried

them on with the boots, and walked in for his mother to give her opinion.

"I think they're okay," he said. "What do you think?"

"Just pull them off. I'll go ahead and do the other two pair the same way." she turned to the sewing machine and checked the bobbin to see if she had enough thread.

The alteration of Willie's pants was all Stacy had worked on since their return from Colorado. She knew David and his dad, Noah, had spent a lot of time at Eric Huckabee's house discussing something, but she had not been given any details.

Stacy started measuring the altered pants with the second pair when David stepped up on the porch. "Stacy, you and Willie come here, we need to talk."

They sat on the back porch in the chairs they used when they were preparing vegetables to can, and when any of the kitchen work was better done outside than in the kitchen. Willie was slow to join them. He sat on the porch step in front of the two chairs. He wondered what the discussion was that required them all to get together.

"This is hard," David said, and paused. Stacy had no idea what he could be talking about. Willie was also puzzled. "Me, Dad and Eric have tried for three weeks to figure out what I learned while I was in Colorado. We came to the conclusion that one of the boys buried in that pile of briars is the rancher's son."

Several minutes passed. Stacy finally asked, "How would you know that?"

David told her the story about the man sending one of his sons to southern Missouri, during the Civil War, to buy livestock. He told how the horse in the rancher's corral was almost identical to the horse Eric had given him, the horse that belonged to one of the four riders.

"His son who is still in Colorado has a saddle and bridle on his horse identical to the one I have on my horse," David said. He felt funny realizing his horse actually belonged to the ranch where he had just bought livestock.

"We have discussed this in every way possible since I got home. And I'm telling you this because we have made a decision."

He went on to say that Eric had brought out the money belt which was the secret that no one was ever able to identify. They had looked for the hat the boy had worn, but they could not locate it. Nate had told them they had removed the boy's hat, but they buried him with his boots on. Nate had stayed with the bodies while Eric went to the barn and got the old canvas wagon covers left from their move from Tennessee. They had stored all but one which they used on trips when they needed to keep stuff in the wagon dry.

Eric told how they wrapped each body separately, and tied rawhide strings around the bodies before they buried them. After all these years he could not remember in what order they had been placed in the ground.

David reached the point he was about to make.

"We're going down to the briar patch that has grown up over those graves, and we are going to see if there's anything left that will make us sure this is Mr. Reynold's son," David said matter-of-factly. "We're going back to Colorado, regardless," he said. "We are returning the money belt."

After a long pause David stood and walked over by Willie leaning against the door post, and said, "I don't want to go out there and tell this man his son is buried along the creek in a briar patch where groundhogs have burrowed over the years, and it has been totally unattended."

He walked across the yard toward the spring. Stacy and Willie followed him without knowing where they were going or why. David stopped. He turned. "I just can't make sense of all this." He didn't expect them to have any answers.

"We're not going to let anybody help us open up the

ground where they are buried. Dad, Eric, and me are just going to do it."

He went back to the house, ending the conversation.

It had been over a week since they started the gruesome task of digging into the burial site. Eric tried to remember the order the men had been placed in the ground. He knew the young man was either the second body as you moved away from the creek, or he was the third. He also remembered how different the young man looked compared to the others. He was neat. His clothes were good. Eric couldn't remember if they buried him with his belt.

When they got to the second body, they found the canvas almost completely gone. There was no flesh or other soft tissue. When they dug toward the feet they found a heel to one boot and the toe for the other one.

They recovered the belt buckle. It was almost identical to the one Willie had bought in the saddle shop in Denver. They only found three or four rib bones. They did not find the skull or any large bones.

"If this was my son, I'd want all of this brought to the ranch in Colorado," Noah said.

The decision was made. They were taking the money belt and the belt buckle, along with the small canvas bag of bones they had recovered from the grave. But did they really know these bones were his?

Willie did not make the trip back to Colorado. He begged grandfather Noah and his dad to let him come along. Eric Huckabee and his oldest son were going with Noah and David Sitton. Noah was in his early 80s, and no longer in good health, but was still able to travel. He hoped.

They took two buggies and headed to West Plains to catch the train to Colorado.

Two weeks earlier they had written a letter addressed to the ranch in Golden, Colorado, saying that they would be there sometime in the next month. They gave no hint why they were making the trip back.

CHAPTER 30

Noah leaned against the corral fence staring at the mountains before him. He was a few miles south and west from Golden, Colorado. When he got to the Reynolds ranch he was amazed at the fertile valley surrounding the huge layout of buildings, barns, corrals, and all the other facilities for running a huge cattle and horse operation.

The mountains still seemed far away. The snow-capped mountains towered high in the sky. He had seen them for a long period of time as they traveled west, starting when they appeared to be something in the clouds on the horizon. He couldn't believe that even now they were still far in the distance.

The trip had been easy, of course. Noah compared it to when they left Wayne County and moved to Arkansas. Then it had taken close to four months just to go some 400 miles. Since they left Big Creek and traveled to Colorado, Noah was not sure how far they had come. It had only been five days.

He had not enjoyed sleeping on the train, but he loved the scenery and eating the food in the dining car. He thought back over his life, and all the change that had happened in such a short time. Now they were here in Colorado to have a discussion with a man who had lost his son in a most unusual situation.

Eric and David went in to visit with Mr. Reynolds and his son. Noah turned and walked toward the house. He didn't knock on the door, he just opened it and slowly entered the huge room. He had never seen a room as plush as this one.

His eyes followed the big ceiling timbers, and he looked at three staircases that exited the room on the ends and in the back. As he turned and looked towards a fireplace, he saw Mr. Reynolds, some years younger than himself, on his knees counting money.

As Noah approached, David and Eric, without saying anything, pointed to a chair for him to sit down. He had already been introduced to Mr. Reynolds and his son before he walked to the corral. He had told them he would join them later.

The rancher finished counting the money. He turned and looked straight at Noah for a minute, maybe longer.

"I just counted all the money," he said in an unsteady voice. "I can't believe he has only spent $420 of the $14,000 I gave him when he left." He stood up and faced his guests from Arkansas.

"Why?" He asked the question without expecting an answer.

Noah stood and joined the rancher.

There was a lot of discussion for the rest of the afternoon. Eric Huckabee had gone into considerable detail about the afternoon of the shooting. He told Mr. Reynolds there had been a lot of robberies and murders for over a year all across northern Arkansas.

"When the Civil War started we were in no man's land,"

Eric continued. He went on to explain that he heard shooting for over an hour before he decided to load the rifles and go into the barn loft to wait and see if they were coming to the Huckabee homestead.

"I started to get down and go to the house for something to eat, when I heard the horses crossing the creek just north of the house." Eric went on to describe how the horsemen rode into the yard, with a big fellow with a scraggy beard and long hair, a coat in tatters leading the way toward the door of the house, yelling for everybody to get out there, he had come to get anything of value.

"Don't hold back anything," he yelled as his partner jumped off his horse, ran to the door, and grabbed Mrs. Huckabee.

Eric described how he shot the fella who grabbed his mother first. He shot the big fellow who was still on his horse second. One of the other riders turned to run away and he shot him. He paused. "I didn't want to shoot your son," he continued. "He sat there during all the shooting, and then he reached for the gun he was wearing, and I shot him."

Eric told how a neighbor brought the one who ran away back, draped across his horse dead.

Noah did not explain he was in Texas fighting with the Confederate Army. Actually, working as a cook during that time, and did not hear about the raids by the Jayhawkers until he got back.

He sat quiet and listened while they tried to explain to a man who lost a 16-year-old boy sent on a mission that had nothing to do with the war. Noah had always wondered, when he got back from Texas and heard the description of the men buried in the field, why there was one odd fellow among them. David had fallen in love with the horse the young man rode, after his uncle Eric had given the horse to him.

They spent the rest of the evening discussing all that had

transpired. Mr. Reynolds looked at the belt buckle for several minutes before he started counting the money. The only reason he counted the money was to see if it was the same money he had gone to the bank in Denver for and placed in the money belt for his son to carry on his trip.

The thing that mystified him the most is how his son managed to keep from being robbed, carrying that much cash, and then joining with a group of three men going through the mountains of northern Arkansas robbing homesteaders.

"There's no good answer," Noah interjected.

They sat quietly while food was set on the table. The five men went to the table and ate. There was no conversation. David was usually capable of giving an explanation and an opinion on any subject under discussion. This time he was quiet, too.

They finished dinner. Mr. Reynolds took them to the guest quarters where the ranch owner always used before he sold it to him. They settled down for the night. There was no further discussion.

It was a bright, beautiful morning when they got up. They went to breakfast. Mr. Reynolds started the conversation.

"I want to thank you gentlemen," he began. "You never had to do what you've done." He paused. "You could have spent the money, never made an effort to find out where the horse came from, or who the young man was that came to your house to rob you." Mr. Reynolds stood up. "I am at peace with losing my son."

He explained the void of not knowing where his son had gone was filled. It explained where he was, but there was no reasonable explanation of why.

They left the ranch house and took a tour of the buildings, and looked at the horses and the prize animals that were one of the best herds in the entire country. They looked at how different ranching was in Colorado compared to moonshining and farming along the creeks in Arkansas. There was no common ground between the two operations. But the Sitton clan and Eric Huckabee left the ranch satisfied they had done the best they could under the circumstances.

CHAPTER 31

Willie sat on the rock extending out from the east side of Big Creek. The rock was a perfect place to sit and fish. He had three smallmouth bass on the stringer beside him. The stringer was a willow limb cut just below a fork. Using the smaller limb to create a fish stringer, he had extended the limb through the gills of the three bass.

He watched the sinker on his line as it bounced along the slick bottom. A minnow, one of the top water minnows with the little white spot between its eyes was on the hook. The minnow was held about a foot above the slick rock by the weight of the sinker. It continued its struggle, trying to come back to the surface. Willie thought about how his grandfather Noah taught him to fish.

As they went into the cane break to cut the first cane pole for Willie to use fishing, Noah explained how he had been taught to set up a cane fishing pole while he was a boy in Wayne County, Tennessee.

He had selected one of the taller and straighter stalks of.

cane. He cut it just below the largest joint in the stalk just above the root wad. After he got the cane pole out of the cane break, he had torn off the leaves up to about seven feet. He had then drilled a small hole through the cane stalk and run the fishing line around the cane pole three or four times before he made a half hitch and pulled it tight.

He then strung out enough line to where it was about two feet longer than the cane pole. He had taken a small threaded nut and run the line through it, tying it off with another half hitch.

"Son, that's your sinker," grandpa Noah said as he handed the pole line and sinker to Willie. "I'm going to let you tie your own hook."

Willie remembered how long it had taken him to tie a knot that was acceptable to his grandfather Noah.

He also remembered when they got through fishing, they had taken the pole back to the cane break and stuck it into the ground with the line, sinker, and hook wrapped around about a foot above where it was stuck in the ground.

"Nobody steals somebody else's fishing pole," Willie remembered him saying as they started towards the house with the four or five sun perch he caught his first time fishing.

It was over three years since they returned from Colorado with the livestock. Eric Huckabee, David Sitton, Willie's dad, and his grandfather Noah had made the trip. The discussions of all the conversations and things which occurred on the trip to Colorado lasted over a year. For the last couple of years the subject was never mentioned.

Willie knew they dug into the graves where the Jayhawkers were buried. He knew his great uncle Eric was very upset, but pleased they had finally solved the mystery. He heard the story of the money and the money belt. He heard the story of the belt buckle, and how much damage the groundhogs and animals had done to the graves during the years following their burial.

He thought about the Levis he was so excited about when he bought them in Denver. He remembered the effort his mother put into cutting them down to fit him. He remembered standing on the same rock looking into Big Creek at his reflection in cowboy boots, Levi pants, and a hat. He was proud he liked the cowboy look.

The boots sat in the corner of his bedroom with the Levis, the belt, and the hat hanging above them. He had not worn them but for a couple of months after they were tailored to fit him. He felt proud going to church at Cedar Grove with his mother, and had gotten out of the buggy expecting people to admire him. When church was over one of the Blair boys began taunting him, making fun of his get up. He knew they all bought the little magazines with the western stories.

He was proud of his look. But the last time he had worn the jeans and the boots he got into a blood fight with one of the McCoy boys at Big Flat. Willie furnished all the blood during the fight. He was done with being a cowboy.

The sinker bobbed hard off the bottom when the top water minnow made its best attempt to get back to the surface. The largest of the bass hiding underneath the rock interrupted it immediately. Willie struggled with the pole as he lifted the extended pole straight up. The fish being immediately in front did not work. The pole bent enough that Willie let the fish flop down on the rock. He dove on top of it to make sure it didn't get off.

Willie left the creek with his four fish after sticking the pole in the cane brake, and he was excited about the fish being fried for supper.

Life was good along Big Creek. Willie Sitton would be 17 at his next birthday. He tried his hand at baseball and found out the only thing he could do well was to hit the ball. His legs were too short. His arms matched his legs. The tall, lanky guys who were good at basketball were all at least a head taller than Willie. He tried basketball over a year ago after going to Campbell to play in a Sunday afternoon game.

He had given up sports, but when he returned to Big Flat a few weeks after the fight with the McCoy boy, the McCoy boy furnished the blood for this fight.

Willie became interested in girls. Noah would deliver a load of moonshine to a fellow named Avey who lived on the Buffalo River. He sold 'shine to the people north of the river in Marion County. Willie had gone with Noah on several trips, and was sweet on Avie's daughter. It turned out to be a bad experience and Willie quit going on the moonshine deliveries.

He had been given a lot of different chores around the Sitton homestead. He had stopped cultivating corn and gone fishing without asking David if he could. But his dad was a lot more liberal with the things Willie could do after his grandfather Noah died just after they got back from Colorado.

Willie was growing up. He had made a trip to the Cedar Creek Mill by himself to have kitchen corn ground. It was the special fine ground his mother wanted for making bread, Johnny cake, and all the other recipes that required cornmeal.

John Rhodes' daughter handled that part of the grinding and packaging at the mill. Willie had met her almost six months before his last trip to the mill. She was 15. Her name was Ellen. He had remembered her as a child, but now she looked different.

A fish fry was planned, and it would be a delicious meal, but what got Willie excited was when he realized he would hitch the mules to the wagon tomorrow and go to the mill.

CHAPTER 32

Willie placed all the corn in the buckboard in the order it was to be ground. The ears of corn with the broad white kernel for the cornmeal was in front next to the seat. The smaller grained yellow corn that was used to make Johnny cake and for other uses was in bags immediately behind. He drove the team faster than usual. He splashed water on the corn while crossing the creek. He remembered his dad absolutely losing his temper when he got to the Cedar Creek Mill with some bags of corn wet. He slowed down. The water on the sacks of corn would dry before he got there. He did not know David had left earlier in the morning and would already be at the mill.

The grinding of the corn was finished. Willie had helped Ellen with everything, including sacking up the meal after it was ground. She had bumped into him once as they carried bags to put in the wagon.

"Oh, excuse me," she said. Her face turned red.

Willie did not answer. For the first time he looked into the eyes of a beautiful young woman.

They finished loading the wagon. Ellen kept three sacks of meal as payment for grinding the corn.

Willie pulled away from Cedar Creek Mill. He had really enjoyed the time he spent there, and Ellen agreed to sit with him if they came to Cedar Grove for any church or other activities.

It had been four years since Willie and Ellen spent that day grinding corn. They now lived in the original cabin Noah built when he settled on the ledge just west of Big Creek. Willie spent his time managing the moonshine, growing crops, including the corn necessary to make moonshine. He was about to upgrade the railroad cross tie making business with a steam powered sawmill.

Willie told his dad it was time to stop making the ties by hand. They owned enough land with enough timber they could justify their own mill. David first objected to spending the money, and said that they were doing well just the way they were doing them.

Ellen was expecting their second child. Their first child was a beautiful blue-eyed girl. Willie's grandmother, with her half Indian blood, had not shown up in his daughter. He didn't have any of the Osage Indian blood showing in him at all. He had not known or questioned about the bloodlines of Ellen's grandparents. They both were a bit surprised when they realized that Ellen's grandmother also had some Osage blood.

They never tried to figure out whether or not they were cousins. There was no way to know because no one was sure about the relationship of the two Indian maidens Jim Campbell and Zeke, the former slave, had married.

It didn't matter on the banks of Big Creek in 1890. Willie heard a lot of stories about all of the things that occurred during and after the Civil War. He knew his dad had probably joined the Ku Klux Klan. He had moved some hay from one side of the loft to the other when he found a white hood and cloak that matched. He put them back and replaced the hay. He knew there were certain questions that were not supposed to be asked.

It was agreed Willie could leave for Springfield, Missouri, to purchase a steam powered sawmill. He talked with John Rhodes' son, Jim, about it. Jim was Ellen's brother; he had bought a store in Big Flat and sold all kinds of goods, including hardware and parts for sawmills. He got most of his supplies by train at the depot in Sylamore.

Jim had catalogs for ordering almost everything, including sawmills. There was a mill in operation on the Marion County side of the Buffalo River. Willie thought the man's name was Davenport. After Jim looked in the catalog and told Willie he thought the Davenport mill was identical to the one in the catalog, he decided to go by there on his way to Springfield.

Willie made the trip. He looked at the steam engine loaded in the wagon. He had purchased a mill identical to the one the Davenports owned. He had no idea the mill would be as big and heavy as it was. The wagon would barely haul just the basic parts to the engine. He would have to get everything else, including the saw and carriage shipped separately.

The Sitton clan had expanded from moonshine, cattle, horses, and timber into a sawmill operation. Searcy County was booming. A railroad was coming from Helena, Arkansas, all the way to Joplin, Missouri. It would pass through Leslie, Marshall, Shirley, and there would be depots every six miles. It would need a lot of cross ties. The Sitton land had the timber and now they were buying a mill.

Willie arrived home with the engine. He had no idea where the best place would be to set up the steam powered sawmill.

Now what?

CHAPTER 33

Willie watched the sawmill as it cut its first cross ties. Wayne Davenport brought his crew from Marion County and spent several days helping set up the mill. They knew what they were doing, and Willie learned a lot from them.

It had taken almost two weeks after he got back with the engine to get the boiler and the rest of the parts. They assembled the carriage on some of the hand-hewn cross ties, and then used cross ties to build the platform for the engine. The saw and gearbox for controlling the carriage had been the toughest part of the mill to align with the saw.

Wayne agreed to leave his men for a week if Willie would give them half of the ties they sawed.

"We could give you all of them," Willie said, "because we would never have gotten this thing together without you."

They enjoyed their time together for the last 10 or 12 days while they put the mill together. Wayne's life was very similar to Willie's. He was the great grandson of a

Davenport from eastern Tennessee. They had made it to Marion County about the same time the Sitton family had settled on Big Creek.

They had done well. They were not in the moonshine business.

"Is it worth fooling with?" Wayne asked Willie one day. After they finished work, and he was trying to figure out how much money could be made making moonshine.

Willie took some time before he answered the question. They had reached the stoop below the shop building, and stood looking at the red-hot forge where they were making more spikes to fasten the cross ties together that were being used to assemble the mill.

Willie walked over and picked up a pair of tongs as he replied to Wayne.

"I don't really know," he finally said. "There's always a market for moonshine somewhere." He paused, then added, "Most of ours is drunk in St. Louis and Memphis."

Wayne listened intently as Willie continued.

"My grandfather was responsible for putting the 'shine business together here, and he knew my grandfather Nate's formula for making good 'shine."

Willie continued to explain to Wayne Davenport how difficult it was to actually make good whiskey. It had become illegal during the Civil War, but so far there had never been any revenue agents in Searcy County.

That had ended their conversation about the moonshine business, and Wayne and his men bunked down in the sleeping quarters in the new barn by the creek next to the Sitton homestead.

The next day as Wayne prepared to leave, Willie assured him his men had learned enough to run the mill on their own. Jim Rhodes, Willie's brother-in-law, Ellen's brother, pulled up in a buckboard hauling a saw blade and other spare parts Wayne had told Willie he needed to keep around because he would need them really often as replacements.

Everyone gathered around, and the men helped unload the wagon. The Davenport men loaded their stuff and were ready to go back to Marion County.

"Willie, get on the wagon with me," Jim said as he climbed up and sat down on the wagon seat.

"I've got a letter addressed to Noah Sitton or Eric Huckabee, and it's from a ranch in Colorado," he said as he pulled a large brown envelope out from underneath the wagon seat. Willie took the letter. The return address was Reynolds Ranch, Golden, Colorado. He did not open it because it was addressed to his grandfather who had passed away, and to his uncle Eric who could no longer see well enough to read.

Ellen finished the supper dishes while Willie and Jim tried to decide whether or not to open the envelope.

"Let's just open it," Ellen said as she went back in the room. She had been listening to all the discussion, and had become more curious with each question they raised about why after all these years they would get a letter from Colorado.

Ellen opened the letter and began to read. It was an invitation from Mr. Reynolds' son for Noah, Eric, and Willie to come to the ranch in Colorado. When Ellen read Willie's name she wondered why he would be invited back since he was not part of the party who had returned the money belt.

She went on to read how Mr. Reynolds had passed away, and that Jason Reynolds now ran the ranch. He invited them to return in the spring, and said his only purpose was to thank them further for the peace of mind his father had after learning what happened to his other son.

David came in just as Ellen finished reading the last of the letter. He looked at Ellen, and he looked at Willie before he turned to Jim Rhodes and asked, "Would you have written that letter?"

"I don't know." Jim stepped outside and looked toward Big Creek. He turned back to answer.

"I have no idea how we are supposed to feel before the war or after the war."

He had been born just after the Civil War ended, but he had heard stories constantly from the time Zeke, the slave, had gained his freedom after a trial in Marshall in 1852. He had heard all the discussions of which side each family should fight on. He wanted it to be over.

"I just don't know what could be accomplished with a trip to Colorado and any discussion about a tragedy that had resulted in this man's brother being buried in a field next to Big Creek," Jim said. He turned, picked up his hat, and started toward his wagon.

For several days the discussion continued of whether or not to go to Colorado. Eric Huckabee said he was not able to make the trip. Willie was anxious to go, and his uncle Samuel, who seldom wanted to do anything other than run the whiskey still, said he would go with him.

Willie began planning the trip.

Ellen did not want Willie to go. She had just found out another baby was coming, and she was not able to do all of her work and take care of Willie's too while he went to Colorado.

CHAPTER 34

Willie sat in the room joining the tack room at the Reynolds ranch. He observed the room and liked the décor. A huge block of wood was used as a table in the center of the room. It was surrounded by six shorter, smaller blocks of wood that served as stools.

Willie sat on one of those stools and placed a bet in a poker game. He imagined a scene where he was part of some of the Western magazines he had read.

The game was Five Card Stud. Willie got three aces in his first five cards. He added a pair of deuces to have a full house. He waited to see if the bet he had placed would be called. The next player to bet had fumbled with all of his money before he asked, "Will you let me call with my violin?"

Willie looked at the instrument and agreed.

They left the ranch early the next morning without really knowing why they had come. Jason Reynolds had thanked them continuously as they prepared to leave.

"I'm so glad you agreed to come," Jason said. He looked at Willie and he looked at his own son who was about Willie's age but more than a head taller than Willie. "I don't know, it just seemed like I would feel closer to the brother I lost in Arkansas if I spent some time with the people who were there."

Willie had trouble understanding that. They rode toward Denver to catch the train. "What could he possibly mean?"

He would have plenty of time to consider the statement during the train ride back to West Plains, Missouri.

The train made good time as it left Denver headed to Wichita, Kansas. Willie slept a couple of hours. He dreamed he was playing poker. In the dream he sat at a poker table. It was a huge red oak stump with six sides flattened out for the players who sat on a cut of a log half as tall as the big wood block in the center. He was dressed as a cowboy. He wore the jeans, boots, and the hat which hung in his closet for several years.

The dream wasn't clear, but was mixed with reality. "Full house," he said as his dreaming mind went back to the reality of when he had three aces and a pair of deuces in his hand.

He knew when he woke up, the dream was like one of the Western magazines he enjoyed reading.

He wondered if the other guy thought there couldn't possibly be any more aces spread around the table. Willie won the fiddle plus a lot of money. And it was the last night they were at the ranch, so there was no chance of him sitting in another game and losing it all back.

He had enjoyed this trip to Colorado. It was, indeed, a different world. In the 1890s the wild west was still alive, and Willie was glad to get back to Arkansas.

Spring had really finished coming out while they were in Colorado. The oak leaves were bigger than a squirrel's ear, the size that grandpa Noah always said was the best for catching the smallmouth Brownies out of Big Creek. The dogwoods were in full bloom, and the Easter lilies had already started to fade.

It was good to be back home. The crosstie mill had been operating for a few years, and the demand for railroad ties was still increasing. Willie thought about how easy it had been the last few years to make money and to live a good life.

The fights about the Civil War had almost stopped. Willie hadn't heard anything about the Ku Klux Klan after he found the hood and cloak in the barn. He was sure it belonged to his dad, but he was not going to ask David about it. The politics had settled down in Searcy County. They had a sheriff who was a friend to 'most everybody in the northeastern corner of the county. And Willie was sure David was paying the sheriff off to keep him from bothering the still.

It seemed, as they tried to pick up and go on after the war, most people were really proud the Union had survived. The money they had could be spent in Denver, Colorado, or in St. Louis; everywhere the dollar was a good thing to have.

The biggest change in the last few years was the establishment of the schools everywhere. Willie had gone through the sixth grade at Cedar Grove, and David had decided that was enough. He could've gone two more years, but he had been more than happy to pick up the duties of running the farm and running the sawmill.

Willie thought about the cars he had seen while they were in Denver. He thought about the chaos of how the horses would run away with the wagons, and he hated the noise some of those automobiles made—more noise than the sawmill, while it is cutting slabs off a log to make a cross tie.

Change is inevitable. Willie thought as he remembered sitting on the porch and listening to the entire Sitton clan talk about things they left behind in Wayne County. He wondered after he got back from Colorado if they felt about Wayne County, Tennessee, the way he felt about Big Creek when he was in Colorado.

He answered the question as he sat watching the shadows climb up the side of the hill on the east side of Big Creek. The sun set a lot quicker in the hollow than it would on the hilltops. The sun had gone behind the snowcapped mountains in Colorado, casting a huge shadow that slowly crept out over the ranch. Darkness seemed to trail closer behind the shadows in Colorado than they did on the waters of Big Creek. Maybe it was because the mountains were so much taller, and the shadow was so much deeper and darker as it came across the ranch.

Willie liked to sit and think in the afternoons between sunset and dusk. In the mornings he was too busy planning his day to become nostalgic like he could after eating supper and sitting in his chair watching the darkness come to the Sitton homestead.

He loved the sounds of the night. The howl of a wolf was seldom heard any more on Big Creek. They had been hunted, along with all the other game, until they were not around. There were still lots of raccoon, very few deer, and unlimited foxes and rabbits. The beaver had been trapped out. There were still a few black bears in the bluffs along the Buffalo River.

Willie adapted to the changes as they occurred. He was happy with Ellen. She was from a different family from the Sitton clan. They were all deeply religious, and Jim Rhodes was one of the leading organizers of the church in Big Flat.

Willie had gone with Ellen when she met Jim and a few other relatives to start a new church in Hickory Hollow. While Willie had not understood the need to do this because she could go by herself to Cedar Grove. It was barely more than half a mile from the Sitton homestead. He had agreed that he would drive her and the girls to Hickory Hollow once a month to meet with that church. Ellen had insisted she would still take the girls to the Sunday school studies at Cedar Grove.

Willie was never sure where he fit in the community. When he went to church he saw some of his very best moonshine customers taking a very active part in the church services.

There was a movement gaining momentum to stop the production of alcohol.

When it became taxed in 1862 during the Civil War, there was hardly any effort to stop the production. It just caused huge distilleries to be built, and a lot of legal whiskey shipped all over the country. When Willie was in Colorado he thought the state of Colorado ran on poker games, women, and alcohol.

Willie no longer thought in terms of money. The Sitton family was run by influence and dedication of the people who farmed and worked for them more than it was the amount of money involved.

"It's my job to make sure everybody has what they need," Willie said. He had heard every other man of influence in the entire area say the same thing.

The Rhodes family, along with a couple of other families became the leaders around Big Flat. The Massey family had become the leaders in the upper end of Big Creek and around Campbell.

Willie wasn't sure how much political power anyone possessed since the war. While the Union had been preserved, the scars left by the war still needed some time to heal.

The sun went down. It was dark. Willie went inside and lit the kerosene lamp. The day would start over tomorrow.

CHAPTER 35

"**I** can't believe it happened," Ellen said. She walked toward her brother, Jim Rhodes, sitting just inside the door of the Sitton cabin.

"One of the Avey boys came to the store yesterday afternoon," Jim said. He added "they looked for Jess all night, but did not find the body until about noon".

Jess Still bought two quarts of moonshine from Willie three days earlier. Willie always sold him the double backs which was the finest 'shine he made.

Jess was not a drunk. He was a good farmer and had taken good care of his family. He had a young wife and three children, and was considered one of the better men living on the north side of Big Creek before you got to the Buffalo River.

"They were all drinking," Jim Rhodes said, "but they didn't consider Jess drunk."

Willie listened, but didn't volunteer that he had sold Jess the moonshine.

Ellen turned. "Did you. sell him any 'shine?" she asked Willie. He didn't answer, just nodded his head.

Ellen began crying. Her brother, Jim, stood and put his arms around her, trying to comfort her. Willie left the room. He did not want to get into a discussion about whose fault it was that Jess had fallen off the bluff while he was 'coon hunting, and lay dead until noon the next day before his body was found.

As the details continued to filter in, everyone from Big Creek to the mouth where it joined the Buffalo River, the Big Flat community, and Cozy Home, blamed Willie Sitton for selling the 'shine causing Jess to fall off the bluff.

I don't see any way that I'm responsible, thought Willie each time he heard the accusations. Ellen pouted. She was not the least bit happy about Willie being accused. She eventually decided it was time to discuss it with Willie.

"Willie, I know you're as good a person as there is in these parts," she began. "It hurts me to listen to people that want to hold you responsible for what happened to Jess Still. Willie stood up and walked to the window, looking out the back of the cabin toward the constantly flowing spring which supplied water for all the needs of the Sitton clan. His mind drifted to all the things they had accomplished, including making a lot of money by selling moonshine.

"Ellen, what if I quit selling it to everybody local, and just produce it for our buyers in St. Louis and Memphis?"

Ellen frowned and stared at Willie. She did not answer his question.

"We don't know any of the people in those cities, and they are going to drink their liquor."

Ellen understood. Willie was saying that selling it to a club in St. Louis or Memphis was different than selling it to their neighbors.

After considerable discussion, Willie agreed he would get all the 'shine out of the barn, and they would ship it to

St. Louis because they were always behind with the amount of moonshine the people wanted in St. Louis or Memphis. It would just make them more money if they stopped selling it to their neighbors.

Word spread quickly that Willie Sitton would no longer sell any moonshine from the barn by the Big Creek bridge.

The bridge had been finished shortly after the turn of the century. Willie built the barn before the bridge was finished. He had found it convenient to intercept people before they crossed the bridge. He moved his blacksmith shop for sharpening plows and other tools to a little shed he built onto the barn. He enjoyed spending the day taking care of the harnesses he stored in the tack room, and in maintaining all the farm tools.

Ellen was comfortable with what he was doing, and he made peace with himself about Jess Still falling to his death while 'coon hunting. No one knew how much the alcohol contributed to his fall. Willie had hunted with Jess, and he could imagine him circling the tree while he held a lantern high above his head as he tried to see where the 'coon was hiding. From the way it had been described to Willie, the side where Jess had fallen off the bluff was very few feet away from the base of the tree.

He knew Jess was backing up to see higher up in the tree when he stepped over the edge. What Willie couldn't figure out was how the fellows hunting with him failed to know he had fallen, and had to backtrack to find him.

"It just don't matter, Willie had concluded.

The railroad ties were no longer in as much demand since the railroad had opened across Searcy County. The price had dropped, and Willie only sawed special orders if they were paid for in advance. He lost a lot of money when he shipped ties to the railroad somewhere in Kansas, and found out later the contractor had diverted them to a railroad being built in west Texas.

Willie had looked at the letter he got ordering the cross

ties, and it looked no different from the ones where he had delivered and been paid with no trouble. But this time he never located the man that sent the letter. And he had sent all those ties to a location where no one admitted to receiving them.

"Just business, just the way things go," Willie had said. But it would not ever happen to him again.

Life. He had just settled in and got back to normal when he went to the house for supper and found his living room full of people. They were having a discussion about a neighbor who had been poisoned on some bad moonshine.

"If Willie had not quit," he heard Jim Rhodes say, "this would never have happened."

Willie stood still. He was shocked. He was blamed for what happened to Jess Still, and now he was being blamed for what happened to another neighbor who had been poisoned on "rotgut." He turned, left the room, and stood on the front porch. He leaned forward, holding onto a post, and looked at the lot where he fed the horses. He had no idea how to respond to the questions being asked.

Ellen joined him. She was followed by their three girls. It had been a good twelve years since the first one was born. Six years later they had the second one, and now they had the third one.

Willie had always wished for a son, but he loved all three of his girls.

"Girls, go back in the house," Ellen said. "I need to talk to your pop."

Willie waited to hear what Ellen had to say.

"I..." Ellen walked up behind Willie, ran her arms around him, and squeezed. She turned away, then suddenly got between Willie and the post he was still holding with his right hand. She stood still. Willie didn't move, either. They watched the horses in the corral fight over the last bit of hay. The horses went to the grain bin and began eating before either Ellen or Willie spoke.

"Ellen, what am I supposed to do?" He did not expect an answer, and he did not get one.

They went back in the house, walked through the room full of people, went to the back porch, and sat in their rockers.

Everybody left without further discussion.

The next morning Willie hooked the mules to the wagon. He loaded enough hay to put the jars of moonshine in, and went to the still just above the mouth of Bratton next to Big Creek. He made the trek around the mountain and back down to the ledge where the still was without seeing anyone. When he got there his Huckabee cousins put the jars of 'shine into the hay without asking any questions.

Willie drove back to the barn and stored the 'shine in the supply room for the still before anyone came by.

It was Jim Rhodes, Ellen's brother, that came by first.

"Willie, I know you made the right choice," he said.

Willie Sitton stood almost in shock. He leaned against the shed where he had built the blacksmith shop. He didn't even try to reply.

Normal is a term everybody uses to describe a situation. Willie was sure what he had gone through the last few years could not be defined as normal.

CHAPTER 36

Normal. A term Willie had heard a lot. The country had tried to get back to normal after the Civil War ended. They had not gone through many problems in Searcy County or around Big Flat.

The fact most of the county's people had been split between the two sides, the Union and the Confederacy, had not lasted more than a few years after the war ended. Willie could not relate to any of that, having been born almost 15 years after 1865.

Noah had passed away shortly after the war. David, though he was still alive, had turned everything over to Willie by the time Willie was 15 years old.

Willie had a knack for a lot of things including making the right financial decisions, or he was just lucky.

While he was confused about the way Ellen and her family accepted his moonshine business when they first got married, he now understood two things had changed in his lifetime. One was the amount of education the children received since schools were established all over Searcy County, and the other was the increase in religion because the schoolhouses had all become houses of worship.

The Sitton clan had supported the building of the school buildings, but they were not church leaders by any stretch of the imagination. Mostly the Sunday schools and the singing of gospel songs were left to the wives and the children.

Willie sat in the tack room mending a set of harnesses.

"Willie, are you doing okay?" The question came from outside. He did not recognize the voice.

Willie went to the door and opened it. His brother-in-law, Jim Rhodes, stood with his back turned. Jim had turned around to look at all the things Willie had built around the barn. There was a hitching post for tying horses. And there was even a feed trough next to the hitching post. Jim tried to imagine how many people could be there with Willie at any given time.

Before he turned to face Willie, he wondered about the rumors he had heard about Willie having poker games inside the small room by the storage area.

"What brings you this way?"

Willie asked the question because he believed it was the first time Jim ever tied his horse up to the hitching rail. Jim did not drink moonshine. Jim did not play poker. Jim Rhodes concentrated on operating the general store at Big Flat, and he was a leader in all the churches throughout the area, and also in the schools.

They sat on the back of the wagon Willie had parked next to the blacksmith shop for repairs. Their conversation became a review of all the things going on throughout the area.

Jim asked Willie about all the land he had acquired during the last few years. Willie explained. It usually started out selling moonshine to someone on credit. It would progress to the point that he loaned cash on the homestead because the people could not make a living on the raw hillside land they had tried to farm.

"Jim, when they come back and want to borrow more money after I've loaned half of what their property could possibly be worth, I make an offer to buy for the amount of money I feel like I can afford to pay." Willie paused, waiting for Jim to reply.

Jim never answered. He just nodded. He now understood the rumors he had heard basically were not true. Willie was not forcing anyone off their homesteads. Jim felt lucky that most of the people came by Big Flat and paid their bill owed at the store before they left. He now understood how Willie had almost 20 sharecroppers living in the old homesteads and farming the land.

"Willie Sitton will keep you busy," the Blair boy said the last time he had come to the store with a list of supplies Willie had sent him to pick up. He was building a fence complete with a water gate across Big Creek just below the mouth of Bratton. Willie had gained title to everything except the Huckabee homestead between the bridge and the mouth of Bratton.

The conversation had not turned to the production of moonshine. Jim had stopped by out of curiosity to find out how Willie gained title to so much property at a time when the economy had been good in Searcy County.

Willie and Jim left the barn and started toward the house to see if Ellen had "a bite to eat," as Willie described it.

Willie ate in silence as he listened to his wife, Ellen, and her brother, Jim, catch up on family gossip and all the other happenings around Big Flat.

"Ellen, the war in Europe is getting bad," Jim said. He referred to the war that had started in the Baltic states and had spread from eastern Europe westward. Ellen and Jim always read every newspaper they could get their hands on. Also Jim had gone to a special finishing school in Memphis and had been admitted to Vanderbilt University before he decided to come home and marry one of the Wallace girls from Big Flat whose great grandfather had started the store years before.

Willie didn't know a lot about the subjects they chose to discuss during the meal. He always concerned himself with the circumstances immediately around him, and the jobs he needed to perform to make sure the Sitton family had all the money and supplies they ever needed.

"There is a sickness that has been diagnosed in Little Rock at Fort Roots," Jim said. "I heard about it while I was at Sylamore waiting for the train from Batesville.

"What is it?" Willie asked. "What is a sickness?"

Jim Rhodes paused, took a drink of the tea Ellen fixed for the meal. He swallowed and looked at Willie.

"Starts, I think, with a high fever and just gets worse," he answered.

Ellen stood up and walked to the stove where she had a cobbler that was cool enough to eat for dessert. She dipped out three servings without asking if anyone wanted the dessert. She had never been turned down for one of her servings of peach cobbler.

"Are they dying from this disease?" Willie finally asked, taking a bite of the cobbler. He reached for the butter, and put a spoonful of butter on top of the cobbler, which melted on the warm cobbler. Willie stirred it with his spoon.

"As I understand it," Jim continued, "there was one tent that had eleven soldiers sleeping in it. Eight of them are dead, and the other three have been sent back home."

A few weeks after that conversation, Jim Rhodes rode back over to see Willie. Once again he found Willie working in the blacksmith shop next to the barn at the end of the bridge.

He sat on his horse for a few minutes watching Willie turning the new bellows he had bought for the blacksmith shop. Willie cranked the bellows, blowing air in under the forge. He took the tongs, turning the horseshoe as it heated red hot. When it was hot enough, he punched holes for the nails.

Jim wished life was as simple as shaping a horseshoe to fit the intended animal.

The news story he read while he was in Marshall was not good. People everywhere were sick. There was now a name for it: the Spanish flu. Jim read that it had started on a hog farm in Kansas, and had been spread by soldiers. While Spain was not involved in the war yet, it had become a staging ground for the armies joining together to fight in Europe.

The Spanish people had been devastated by the disease.

CHAPTER 37

Jim finished giving Willie the news of the war and the flu epidemic, which it was now called. They sat quietly, listening to the water of Big Creek rushing over the shoal directly underneath the bridge. They went to the pier that had been poured to support the cables making the swinging bridge. They sat facing the creek. Their discussion stopped when they realized they were overwhelmed with questions and no answers.

Jim's horse took him back to Big Flat at a good speed. He had been gone all day and was anxious to get home.

It'd been almost three months since Jim had stopped by to see Willie. The sickness had made it to Big Flat, and people had died from it. But it stopped for some reason and moved on. Willie thought they were spared because very few of the soldiers caught it, and had not infected people when they came home.

There was an exception. Ellen lost six relatives in one week.

Willie turned nostalgic. He spent several days in

discussions with all the families along Big Creek. He visited with all of his farm help, and he talked to everyone who worked with moonshine.

He felt it was necessary to take a look back at what they had accomplished, and to try to get a plan together going forward if prohibition became law. The temperance movement gained a lot of momentum. It had two purposes: stop the production of alcohol and give women the right to vote.

Willie had never been political. Willie had never been religious. Willie had just been Willie, a young man born on Big Creek who enjoyed reading the magazines about out West. He loved the trip to Colorado. He'd about given up on ever learning to play the fiddle he won in the poker game.

When he built the barn he added the room in the front, he had used a big block of wood as a table, and six shorter cuts around it for stools to sit on. He never told anyone he had tried to recreate the same room he played poker in while in Colorado.

Willie had never been concerned about people's opinions until Jess Still fell off the bluff. He made the changes Ellen asked him to make. He changed again after the rotgut being sold almost killed a good friend. He went back to selling the best moonshine he could make.

He played poker with all of his neighbors, and they drank moderately. They never had a brawl or any kind of fight that drew attention to what they did.

The worst incident Willie remembered happening in the barn was when a fellow who could not pay his mortgage came to the barn trying to figure out a way to get out of his debt.

"I'll give you $150 more," Willie said. "That's what you owe me on your property." He waited for the man from Mississippi to answer him. He had sold him 'shine on credit. He loaned him $150 cash and took a mortgage on his farm. The man had cleared some land that should have been left in timber. He tried to plant crops on gravel hillsides that were too steep and on land atop ledges where the soil was too thin to grow anything.

Willie felt sorry for him. He was a hard worker, and had spent three years clearing the land, building a house, and he had spent all the money he had when he got there. Willie now offered him $150 cash, and he could leave.

"Could I just cut you high card for my debt?" he asked.

Willie looked at the deck of cards laying on the stump that served as a table. He picked them up. He thought about it. He shuffled them and spread them out on the table. The man from Mississippi drew a card. Willie drew a card. The Mississippi man turned his card over. The five of spades. Willie turned his card over. The jack of diamonds.

Willie watched as the man put both hands on the table palms down. He watched as his head began to bob, as if he might be crying and sobbing.

Willie counted out $150 and laid the money between the man's hands on the table.

"Go to Jim Rhodes at Big Flat. He will make a deed to the property for me. Sign it and leave it at the store," Willie said. "That card deal was no way to solve a problem. I want you to be able to get back home to Mississippi where you belong, and I don't want you feeling like I have taken advantage of you."

The man picked up the money and left.

Willie walked to the back of the barn. He looked at the bluff just east of what became known as "the swimming hole" on Big Creek. Willie wasn't sure why circumstances seemed to always bring to him something he was not ready to deal with.

Willie and Ellen sat on the back porch watching the water flow through the channels Noah had created many years ago. His grandfather had set in place everything that Willie had used to create the life that he and Ellen enjoyed.

Life was good.

CHAPTER 38

February 1920. Willie had never been too concerned about the time of the year, or the date. He always enjoyed the seasons. Winter was probably his favorite, his favorite month was probably February. He liked the warm sun and longer days of February. It seemed to him the most relaxing month of the year. It was too early to start the crops, but it was time to start planning what would be planted in each field.

He traveled to all the homesteads he possessed, and talked to all of the sharecroppers about their plans for his next crop. He didn't usually object to what anyone wanted to farm. He always paid a standard price for the corn, whether it would be used to feed livestock, for meals and food for the table, of if it was of high enough quality to make moonshine.

Willie finished repairing a plow handle and placed it back on the plow. He looked up and saw the Searcy County sheriff riding toward the barn.

The sheriff was Joe Carson, and he was well into his second term. Willie had not met him until almost a year ago. The Huckabees took care of the sheriff, and Willie didn't really want to know how they worked it out concerning the moonshine.

"Good morning," said Willie as Joe Carson dismounted from the big bay mule. The sheriff had to have a large animal to ride because he was well over six feet tall and probably weighed 230 pounds. Willie didn't like to stand close and talk to the sheriff because it made him feel like a midget.

Willie told everyone he was 5'7". But when Ellen had measured the height of their girls, they talked Willie into letting them measure him. Willie stretched as much as possible, but he could not convince them he was 5'7" tall.

He never admitted it, but he left the house the next morning feeling short. Too short. He developed a complex.

Joe Carson tied up the mule and walked as close to Willie as Willie would let him. Willie stepped up on a stool he used when he put shoes on horses and mules. The little stool was probably 16 inches tall. It gave Willie the height he needed to look down at the sheriff as he talked with him.

"Willie, you know the new law passed last month, don't you?" Joe referred to the prohibition act that passed in January, 1920.

Willie thought for a minute. He had wondered while all the talk was going on, about making alcohol illegal, what effect it would have on making moonshine, which was already illegal.

Joe Carson, as County Sheriff, had his office in the courthouse at Marshall. Leslie was the largest town in Searcy County. St. Joe was actually bigger than Marshall, and several other communities had their own marshals and constables. Joe's job primarily was serving warrants, and bringing in people for trial in Circuit Court. Big Creek was closer to Big Flat than any other community of any size.

All the little schoolhouses scattered around through the hills had a name, and some were considered a community.

Joe had ridden the mule from a corral where Long Creek and Davis Creek came together to form Big Creek. He always drove the sheriff's car to that point and then rode the mule to wherever else he needed to go. The sheriff seldom ever traveled along Big Creek.

"I don't know what to believe about how much law will be enforced out in the hills of Arkansas and Missouri," the sheriff said as he walked closer to Willie, which made him uncomfortable. Willie stepped off the stool and went inside the barn. The sheriff followed him.

They sat down on the stools and leaned their elbows on the stump table. The sheriff was now looking down at Willie who was five feet away from him across the table.

"I don't intend to make any changes to what I am doing now," Willie finally said. He didn't tell the sheriff that his biggest customers in St. Louis and Memphis had asked him to make every drop of moonshine possible, or that they would pick it up at a barn they rented just north of Calico Rock on the White River.

Willie had been told they would pay in advance for whatever amount they got. They would leave the money for the next batch before he ever delivered it. Willie made a deal with a distant cousin who farmed in the valley and owned the barn to handle his money.

Joe Carson stood and said, "Willie, I know you don't do many things where you're directly involved." He walked around to the side of the table where Willie sat. "I expect you've already got it figured out what you're going to do." At the door he turned back. "My dad made a deal with your dad, no it was actually with your grandfather, Noah, long before I was ever sheriff, and they agreed to not bother you or your family while you make moonshine."

Willie followed Joe outside. Joe untied the mule and started to mount before Willie said anything.

"I appreciate you coming by," he said, "but the only thing I wonder is if the federal people will show up." He hesitated, then asked, "What will we do then?"

It had been over six months since Joe Carson had visited Willie at the bridge.

It had been one of the best years Willie ever had with the moonshine business. They bought a boxcar load of grain from Kansas and hauled it by wagon from the train depot at St. Joe to the still on Big Creek. Willie didn't necessarily like the quality of the 'shine they had made from that grain. But doubling the price and making it without any care for quality had been very profitable.

One morning in July he had gone to the barn, found the door standing open, and when he went inside all the 'shine he kept for his neighbors was gone. He got a chain and padlock, and cut holes through the doors where he could lock every one of them. He now kept the shed locked.

He walked slowly up the bank across the patch of land where the potatoes had already been dug. The turnips were beginning to come up. He went on to the house.

Ellen and the girls were trying on the new dresses she had just finished.

There was excitement on Big Creek. They were going to church in Big Flat next Sunday. Willie had agreed to take the buggy that had two seats, and would pull it with the team of black horses he had bought when he bought the buggy. For the age that was fast becoming the day of the automobile, Willie enjoyed driving that buggy. He would be ready to make the trip come Sunday.

CHAPTER 39

September was Willie's favorite month to ride in the new carriage. It was too big to call a buggy, and with four wheels and a soft spring suspension, the ride was smooth even along the rocky road that followed a hollow away from Big Creek.

The wagon road had been developed along the ledge up each hollow before turning and coming back out to the edge of the main hollow. Willie called each one of the turns "gooseneck turns."

The girls enjoyed the buggy ride. Ellen had always taken the single seated buggy bought years ago in Springfield, Missouri. It was pulled with a mule or horse, and was a much rougher ride, and slower than the new buggy with the gaited team.

The ride became really smooth when they got to the level land of Big Flat.

The road, while well packed with a combination of sand and clay, did not have the rocks and chuck holes of the rough trail along the rocky hillsides east of Big Creek.

They passed by several well-kept homesteads, and there were several good herds of cattle showing signs of the bloodlines Willie and Noah brought back from Colorado. The farmers had all done well since the end of the Civil War. The houses, for the most part, had been reroofed with the corrugated metal roofing which was much easier to maintain and seldom leaked.

Most of the rail fences had been replaced with a web wire some 38 inches tall, and two barbed wires above that. The fencing had made it much easier to keep the cattle from raiding the crops and destroying the gardens. The fence posts were either cedar, locust, or chinquapin. Willie remembered Jim talking about how much wire and fence staples he sold at the store. He had started going to a hardware store in Batesville, Arkansas, and buying the wire and staples at a better price than he could get by ordering direct from either Springfield or Memphis.

They arrived at the church, and Ellen complained that they were late because they had trouble finding a place to park the buggy. Eventually Willie let Ellen and the girls out, and he took the buggy up to the store and tied the horses to the hitching post in front of the store.

As Willie walked back across the town branch and started to climb the little knoll back up to the church, he noticed all the houses that had been built since the last time he had come to Big Flat.

Willie got to the churchyard and looked around. He didn't see any men gathered together underneath the tree to visit while the women and children went inside for church. He decided to go on in and sit with Ellen and the girls if he could.

Jim Rhodes, Ellen's brother, was the superintendent of Sunday schools and usually conducted the song service. Willie sat down on the end of the pew after Ellen took their youngest and sat her on her lap to make room for Willie.

Willie actually enjoyed being in church. He hadn't been since they had gone to Cozy for Easter service back in April. Willie usually went to church a couple times a year. This was the second time he had gone in and sat through the entire service.

He listened as Jim Rhodes gave a description of his last trip to Batesville to buy supplies. Jim told the story of how he had been invited by a Mr. Carr, who operated the hardware store, to attend church with him on the Wednesday night. Jim spent quite a bit of time describing a young man from Wayne County, Tennessee, who had offered a testimony which had turned into a full-blown sermon.

Willie did not understand the excitement of the story or how Jim seemed to be carried away with the details of his description of the young preacher. Jim went on to talk about having visited with the young man the next morning when he placed his order at the hardware store. According to Jim it was an interesting experience.

"He was different than anyone I've heard before," Jim said. He continued his elaborate description of the young man, and talked about how easily he was able to speak, his height, his smile, and on and on. He finally ended with, "I have written him a letter asking him to come and visit us here in Big Flat." Jim ended the morning service by saying, "I hope he comes."

While driving the carriage back to Big Creek, Willie commented, "Jim got carried away talking about that young minister."

Ellen didn't answer. Her frown told Willie that she did not appreciate his opinion about Jim.

When Ellen got in the carriage she said, "Let's hurry home, the girls are hungry."

They went home without making the usual stops to visit friends and relatives around Big Flat.

Willie learned later that while he had parked the buggy,

and while he went to get the buggy after church, Ellen had heard criticism about how Willie had expanded the farm, and about how much moonshine he made. She had also heard stories about the card games in the barn.

During the next several days Willie heard bits and pieces of all those conversations. Every buyer of 'shine who came by the barn told him a little bit about the stories. Basically, it was the contradictory lifestyle of the moonshiners along Big Creek and other areas around the Buffalo River with the farming being done in the Big Flat community and the rest of the area.

Over the years row cropping of cotton and some tobacco had become very profitable after the timber boom ended. There was now a cotton gin in Big Flat, Leslie, and Marshall. And they were building one somewhere else. Willie couldn't remember where for sure.

Willie wasn't bothered long about the criticism. Ellen seldom ever criticized him or questioned what he did to make money. He quit giving it any thought after a few days, and got busy with the fall harvest, which included making molasses. It was one of his favorite things to do. He was excited about this year's crop, and spent the next few weeks with the harvest.

CHAPTER 40

Willie ordered several cases of quart jars, and Ellen picked them up at the store in Big Flat. He always ordered a lot of jars for the molasses, never worrying about ordering too many. He could always sell 'shine in them if there were any left over.

He enjoyed the harvest. Newt Blair, his new neighbor, helped cook the molasses. Newt was good at it, and made sure all the green foam was skimmed off early in the process and was not stirred in.

The cane grown along the fields next to the creek always turned out darker than the cane grown on the bench land and the fields above the creek. He liked the color of them. The sandy soil made the cane sweeter, not as bitter as the darker molasses from the cane field next to Big Creek. Ellen liked the batch when the juice from the creek got low and they mixed in the smaller, thinner cane grown on the sand field.

Newt Blair had a lot of honeybees. He started mixing

molasses and honey together, and cooked up a toffee with peanuts added in. Mrs. Blair called it honey brittle.

When you added the molasses, the honey, and all the game that was harvested following frost, it made for a lot of festive meals along Big Creek.

Willie heard some gossip after they started the harvest, about what was said during the trip they had made to church at Big Flat. He had looked over the congregation. He didn't really know over half of the men in church that Sunday morning. He recognized only a couple who had bought 'shine at the bridge.

After the harvest was finished, Jim brought the rest of the jars that Willie had ordered and set them on the front porch of the house. The Huckabee boys came by and picked them up without asking Willie. They knew all the excess jars would go to the moonshine still.

Jim stayed and visited with Ellen. He told her the new preacher had come, and was coming back to be the new pastor of the three churches. He would preach the first Sunday of the month at Hickory Hollow just a couple miles from the Sitton homestead. He would preach the third Sunday of the month at Cozy Home several miles to the north of the Big Creek bridge. He would preach the second and fourth Sundays at Big Flat, and would live in the parsonage across from the church.

Ed Tice was his name.

It seemed to Willie that for a month every time he heard anybody say anything, it was about the young man and his wife, Liz, and something they had said or done.

Ellen and the girls even asked him to go to church at Cozy Home. It would be easy to go by himself riding a mule, but he could not imagine taking the carriage there. They would have to go up the hollow all the way to Rock Creek, and then come back along the ridge four miles to the Cozy Home schoolhouse.

Willie decided that the next Sunday when the new

preacher came to Hickory, they would go.

Willie tied the horses to the hitching rail next to the road. The two rails closest to the Hickory Hollow schoolhouse were already full of horses and mules when they got there.

Willie looked toward the big oak tree where he usually sat with the other men while the women and children went inside for church. His friends were there, and had already started their usual whittling of cedar with the sharpest knives in the area.

Willie was no different than any other man around Big Creek. He took pride in his pocket knife, and he had all three blades sharpened for a particular use. The big long blade he used to cut limbs or any other heavy cutting. The second blade he kept sharp enough to peel an apple with the peeling really thin but thick enough that it would fall off in one piece when he finished peeling that apple. The last blade was special. It had to be sharp enough to shave the hair on your arm, or you couldn't cut the fine little shavings off of a whittling stick, and have them curling properly in a pile as you whittled.

He sat down, retrieved his stick from his pocket, and began whittling. He watched the other fellows. Every one of them were able to cut good-looking shavings.

They all heard the new preacher as soon as he got to the podium and prayed. The Hinkle man stopped whittling and turned toward the building, listening intently to the prayer. Willie paused and listened for a couple of minutes. He had never heard a voice that clear and distinct.

As the preacher began preaching, they whittled in earnest, and tried to talk about the crops and other subjects like they usually did during the church services. They eventually stopped whittling and listened to the closing prayer.

Willie stood up and leaned against the tree. He had never seen this new preacher. He had heard the name enough times, though. Ed Tice was almost a constant on everybody's tongue. He watched as all the children came out of the building. He waited to see Ellen come out and walk over to where the girls stood watching the door with everybody else.

Finally, the new preacher came out of the building along with Jim Rhodes. He walked in stride with Jim as they headed toward Ellen.

A young lady had come out before the two men, and Willie decided she had to be Liz. He thought she was beautiful, but he didn't mean that in any way except admiration for the neat, well-dressed young woman.

Willie's thoughts switched to being back in the blacksmith shop that afternoon. He needed to sharpen all the tools before putting them away for the winter. He liked to have his tools stored and ready for spring.

The visiting on the churchyard lasted longer than usual. Willie wasn't sure how long. He eventually shook hands with the new preacher.

Willie couldn't decide how he felt about all the attention the man was getting. Nor could he explain the pleasant voice that greeted him with, "So you're Willie." The preacher paused and then said, "You're Ellen's husband, and the father of these three beautiful girls."

Their eyes locked. Surprisingly, they both saw friendship. The moonshiner had met the preacher.

ABOUT THE AUTHOR

Sam Pemberton was born on Bratton Creek, at an old homestead that hadn't changed much since the pioneer days. The year was 1944. Pemberton graduated from Big Flat high school. After their graduation in 1962, Sam married the love of his life, Patricia Treat.

He has worked construction in the drywall trade for most of his life. Sam presently lives in the beautiful Ozarks and continues in construction, as well as developing a new adventure called The Gathering Place in Big Flat, Arkansas, which is a restoration of the old building that is referred to in the novel as the store. He hopes you'll stop by sometime.

www.ingramcontent.com/pod-product-compliance
Lightning Source LLC
Chambersburg PA
CBHW071846220626
47052CB00012B/854

* 9 7 8 1 9 6 0 4 9 9 0 8 0 *